"Well, now, Miss Genevieve, that is a good question. Why would I want to see you again?"

He scratched his head and pretended to consider it. Actually, the only trouble he had with answering was how much to say and what to say first, but he'd never tell her that. Before he could sort out his thoughts and give her a brilliant answer, she had the audacity to turn around and walk away.

"Never mind," she said with a wave of her hand. "I'm sure I will see you around. Good-bye, Mr. Breaux."

For a split second he thought of following her, of using his considerable charm to woo her into continuing their conversation. He certainly had no trouble making small talk with the ladies. Then his brain caught up with his pride, and he stopped. Better to approach this situation with care—and a little planning.

Why, he wouldn't hack at just any old oak tree in order to get lumber for a chair or cut down the closest pecan tree to find wood for a table. No, he would choose the best trees, take time to study them, and then treat them with care.

The same would go for Genevieve Lamont. Taking the time to approach her carefully would be his plan. He would study her and figure out just the right way to get to know her.

For, like a piece of fine furniture, she obviously had great value.

KATHLEEN Y'BARBO is a native Texan with a marketing degree from Texas A&M University. The former treasurer of American Christian Fiction Writers, Kathleen is also a member of Romance Writers of America, Writers Inspiration Network, Words for the Journey, and the Author's Guild. She frequently speaks on the craft of writing to schools and writing groups and teaches creative writing on the college level.

Books by Kathleen Y'Barbo

HEARTSONG PRESENTS
HP474—You Can't Buy Love
HP529—Major League Dad
HP571—Bayou Fever
HP659—Bayou Beginnings

Bayou
Secrets

Kathleen Y'Barbo

Heartsong Presents

To Sharen Watson, who blesses me beyond measure and gives me and so many other words for the journey. Wherever your travels take you, may you always find blessings there—and an endless source of words for your own journey.

A note from the Author:
I love to hear from my readers! You may correspond with me by writing:

Kathleen Y'Barbo
Author Relations
PO Box 721
Uhrichsville, OH 44683

ISBN 1-59310-799-4

BAYOU SECRETS

one

Genevieve Lamont Gallier stood behind the cash register and toyed with the locket at her neck. Not that anyone called her by that name. Genevieve Lamont had served her well for most of her twenty years, and she saw no reason to turn from it now.

In a few minutes, the doors of the five-and-dime would be thrown open, and her workday would officially begin. Unlike the other employees who slipped in the back in time to see customers coming in the front, Gen arrived early. Those precious few moments of quiet before the store opened were what made her day bearable.

Thank You, Lord, for Your provision and mercy. May I be Your hands and feet today, and may my mouth speak only what is pleasing to You, even when my irritation gets the better of me.

She looked up at the main source of her irritation, her boss Lester Bonfils, currently perched on a stool at the ice-cream counter. Dorothy Barnes, the soda fountain's usual operator, had wisely waited until the last moment to take her place behind the counter. Currently, the young woman was studiously cleaning soda glasses on the farthest end of the area.

While Gen watched, Lester sopped up the remains of a plate of scrambled eggs with a triangle of buttered toast, then stuffed the entire thing in his mouth. When he wiped his mouth with his shirttail, Gen looked away. The man was a good fifteen years older than she—thirty-five, at least—with a belly the size of Mother's prize-winning watermelon, yet he strutted around the five-and-dime like a banty rooster in a henhouse. In recent weeks, Gen had become Lester's favorite hen, and only the most adamant of refusals had kept the lecherous storekeeper at bay.

5

Lester strolled past the register, twirling his keys and sucking the last taste of his breakfast off his fingers. He caught her staring and winked. Gen refused to react. She'd learned early on that anger piqued Lester's interest just as much as a sweet smile.

Sorry, Father. Where was I? Oh, yes, make me a better person today, Father. I know I've got a long way to go, but if You don't mind, could You fix me up so's You're happy with the result? Mother, she isn't much pleased with me, and Big Mama, well, she doesn't say much one way or the other. Take care of them, Lord, and watch over my precious one. I give this day to You. All I ask is that You help me through it. Oh, and if You don't mind, make it go by fast, what with today being Friday and all.

"You praying again, girl?"

Gen swung her gaze to meet Lester's stare. Rather than respond, she turned to straighten the stack of receipts beneath the counter.

"You see that clock on the wall over there?"

"Yes, sir," she said without looking up.

"What does it say?"

Gen blinked and narrowed her eyes. Seeing things at a distance had always been a problem. Mother said she ought to get some glasses, but thus far Gen had managed just fine without them. Thankfully, the hands on the store clock were black and the numbers large.

"It says nine o'clock straight up, sir."

"That it does." Lester gave the keys one last toss. "And you know what that means, Miss Lamont?"

"The store is open for business."

"That's right." He stabbed the key into the lock and gave it a turn. "Business, Miss Lamont, not prayer. This ain't a church. Well, good morning, Reverend Brunson, Mrs. Brunson," he said as he stepped back to let the parson enter.

Did I say, Amen, Father? 'Cause I've already forgotten if I did, but then I've been a mite forgetful ever since. . . Well, You know, and that's what counts. And just in case I didn't, Amen.

Lunch came and went, but Gen skipped hers so she could finish work a half hour early. Lester didn't much care for the girls trading shifts and working each other's lunches, but he rarely noticed.

Her roommate, Betty, slipped into Gen's spot behind the cash register. "You be sure and tell your mama I've been praying for her."

"I will," Gen said. *Or rather, I'll try. Not that Mother's generally willing to stay in the same room with me anymore.*

Betty gave her a hug, then pressed something into Gen's palm. She opened her hand to find a folded five-dollar bill.

"Oh, honey, no," she said as she thrust the money back at Betty. "That's a fortune. I can't take this. Absolutely not."

"I don't see how you have a choice, Genevieve Lamont. I've gone and handed it to you, and I don't plan to take it back." She feigned irritation. "Now are you going to stand there and tell me you don't need that?"

Gen tried to think of a reason. Unfortunately, Betty knew too much to believe any of them. She'd seen Gen patch her two good dresses and go without lunch to put away bus money and a little bit extra to take back home to the bayou.

At least Betty didn't know the full extent of what awaited Gen back in Latanier.

Eyes misting with tears, Gen offered a heartfelt thanks then slipped out the door and headed back to the little room at the boardinghouse where her packed suitcase sat on the narrow bed nearest the wall. Every Friday, she dreaded getting on the bus, and every Sunday afternoon, she felt the same about returning to the city.

Was it possible to be torn between two worlds?

She trudged up the two flights of stairs to the third-floor room she now called home and threw open the door. Trying not to think, Gen changed into her traveling dress and comfortable shoes, then snatched up her bag. She counted her money—just enough to buy a bus ticket and a few things for the folks back home—and gave thanks that the Lord had seen fit to provide her with a job. So many people were out of work nowadays, and she did not take the blessing of a job lightly.

She leaned against the wall and slipped Betty's five-dollar bill into her shoe. *Thank You, Lord. And just when I thought Mother would have to do without her medicines. . .Well, Your timing is always perfect.*

At the door, she turned to cast a glance at the sparsely furnished room and sighed. Who would have believed her life had come to this? She might be a month shy of twenty-one, but in her heart she'd become an old woman.

It was the secret she carried that aged her so—leastwise that's what Big Mama claimed. That and the choices she'd made.

Actually, one choice.

Glancing at the nightstand, Gen noticed she'd forgotten her Bible. In four steps, she crossed the room to retrieve her lifeline to the Lord and placed it atop her things in the suitcase.

As she turned quickly, she caught sight of herself in the mirror. Even though it was cloudy and cracked with age, there was no denying what the mirror told her.

She stepped closer and peered at the image that blinked back. Gen didn't need glasses to know the woman in the mirror was not the same person who had stepped off the bus from Latagnier two months ago.

I don't even recognize myself.

At the bottom of the stairs, Gen stopped and touched the locket at her neck, a habit that served to remind her of who she was and what she'd left behind. A moment later, she set off down the sidewalk toward the bus station. The clock on the town square read twenty minutes after five, plenty of time to make a detour before the 5:40 bus left.

She crossed the street and veered into Mulotte's Grocery. Mother always did like lemon sours. *Maybe this time she'll accept them.*

Last time she'd offered a gift, her mother had thrown it out the upstairs window.

A little time had passed, nigh on two weeks since she'd seen her. Maybe the woman had settled her anger a bit, possibly reconsidered her decision to cut her only daughter out of her life.

Or maybe she would take her locked-up feelings to the grave. There was no telling with Mother.

Gen tossed the bag of sours into the little basket and moved farther down the aisle. A few cans of evaporated milk and a container of oatmeal with the extra bonus of a free drinking glass inside went in after them, and her money was almost spent. She got all the way to the end of the aisle and turned back up the next before she found the treat Big Mama loved so well: a package of freshly made pork cracklings. And they were on sale.

"She'll fuss, but I'm buying them anyway."

"Who will fuss?"

Turning toward the sound, Gen let the cracklings fall. The tall gentleman snagged the bag and settled it atop her other purchases. As he moved nearer, a familiar face appeared. The fellow must be one of the Breaux boys. He certainly had that look about him.

Funny. For the life of her she couldn't place which one.

"Remember me?"

Uh-oh. "Sure," she said as she pressed past him to head for the cash register. "You're a Breaux from Latanier, right?"

"Yes, ma'am, I am." He caught up and thrust his hand toward her. "Ernest Breaux, Miss Lamont. I'm the eldest of the bunch."

The eldest. No wonder she didn't remember him by name. By the time she arrived at the little Latanier schoolhouse on the edge of the Bayou Nouvelle, Ernest had already finished his education.

"I'm really sorry," she said as she pried her hand loose from his grip, "but I'm in a hurry. Nice to see you again."

Not that she actually saw him that clearly. Maybe she ought to take Mother's advice and get that eye examination after all.

❧

Ernest tried not to let his deflated ego show. The Lamont girl seemed to look right through him. Why, he'd been something of a man about town back in Latanier. Maybe she liked big-city men.

Well, then, she would like him for sure once she knew he'd shaken off the dust of that little bayou town and made his home right here in New Iberia. Actually, he slept in a modified storeroom with two other sawmill employees, but he'd have a real place here soon enough.

Yes, he was a city man for sure.

A city man with a car. And not just any car.

No, sir. His was a 1927 Model T roadster bought used from his boss at the sawmill after the engine went bad. The black beauty set him back almost a year's worth of salary, and the engine still wasn't what it ought to be, but every time he sat behind the wheel, he had no doubt it was worth the cost. After all, what did he have to save his money for? He was footloose and fancy-free, a single man with only himself to answer to.

Well, himself and the Lord.

"Hey, Miss Lamont, wait up."

She didn't appear to hear him. Ernest trailed her outside and looked both ways before spotting her heading east with a suitcase in one hand and a small black handbag in the other. While he watched, she crossed the street and disappeared around the corner.

Catching up to her in the roadster turned out to be easy; getting her attention, now that was another matter altogether. He idled up behind her and let the engine purr as he steered the car to the curb just ahead of her.

Ernest ran a comb through his hair and replaced his cap, then prepared himself for the attention he knew he would garner once Miss Lamont saw his means of transportation. In the rearview mirror, he saw her approach.

He checked his appearance once more and tilted his cap for a rakish effect. Pretending to study his nails, Ernest bided his time.

Any minute now, Genevieve Lamont would come strolling

by. All he had to do was be patient. Just another second and. . .

What in the world? The woman in question strolled past as if he were invisible.

Well, that just wouldn't do.

"Miss Lamont, excuse me." No reaction, except to possibly pick up a little speed. He tried again. "Hello, Genevieve Lamont."

This time she slowed just a bit then hurried toward the bus station. Ernest jumped out of the roadster to set off after her on foot, reaching the bus station door just before she reached to open it.

She looked up at him with wide eyes rimmed with thick lashes. Those eyes narrowed. "*Mr.* Breaux. If you don't mind, I have a bus to catch."

"A bus? Why take the bus when that beauty is at your disposal?"

Ernest stepped away from the door to point toward his prize possession. When he turned around to gauge Miss Lamont's reaction, she was nowhere to be found.

two

Ernest finally found the Lamont girl at the ticket counter. She stood behind an elderly couple whose only luggage was a covered basket that contained a small yapping dog. He tipped his hat, which set the dog barking even louder.

Rather than call her name and risk not being heard, Ernest strolled over and tapped her on the shoulder. "Going my way?"

Miss Lamont gasped and dropped her suitcase, sending it crashing. When the cheap cardboard hit the floor, the latch opened and a weekend's worth of clothing spilled out.

"I'm so sorry," he said as he bent to retrieve her lost garments. "I didn't mean to scare you."

A look of horror crossed her pretty features. Ernest followed the direction of her gaze. "Oh, I, well. . ." He let the lacy item drop into her bag, then quickly stuffed the rest of the items in after it. The latch safely shut once more, Ernest jammed his fists into his pockets, his face flaming.

An eternity passed, and she still stared. Ernest looked past her to the wall where the clock's big second hand ticked off a few more seconds. Finally, he grasped at the first thought crossing his brain.

"So as I was saying, would you happen to be heading back to Latanier today, Miss Lamont?"

At first he thought she might turn around and pretend she hadn't heard the question. She sure didn't look excited about the prospect of sharing the road with him.

"Yes, I am," she finally said as she checked the latch on her bag. "Why?"

"Because. . ." Ernest paused. Why indeed? "Well, because I am, too."

Even though he could barely wait to show Papa and the

others the roadster, he had intended to put off visiting the family until he'd had a chance to work on it a bit. The Acadian beauty didn't need to know that. Besides, Mama *was* always after him to spend more time at the home place, and Papa would be tickled to watch while he worked on the big engine.

He studied her while she fidgeted and frowned. It looked like he'd be going home alone, if he went home at all.

"That's nice of you," she said. "But really, I couldn't put you out like that. It's too much trouble."

"It's no trouble at all. Shall we?"

Ernest reached for her suitcase, then attempted to link arms with Miss Lamont. Turned out the girl was faster than she looked. Somehow she managed to grab her bag and skedaddle away before he could blink twice.

Ernest watched her tromp back into the line, which had now grown by two middle-aged women, three badly behaved young'uns, and a rapscallion of a man who gave Miss Lamont a look that should have earned him a slap.

When the fellow turned around and began to say something to her, Ernest knew he must take action. After all, how could a gentleman like himself possibly allow a sweet young thing like Genevieve Lamont to board a bus where her virtue might be in peril? He reached her side in time to hear the man in question lean far too close and inquire as to whether Genevieve "had a man back home."

The look on her face sent Ernest into action. The way he figured it, he could either deck the cad or rescue the damsel in distress. He didn't have to think too long on that choice.

"Well, there you are, honey pie," Ernest said. "I was wondering where you got off to." He looked straight into the man's eyes and gave him a stare that would wither a cactus. "Excuse us, won't you?"

This time, he led her out of the bus station without protest. At the curb, she stopped short and wrestled her elbow from his grip. Ernest glanced back to see if the fellow had followed them.

It might not do to draw blood in front of such a delicate creature, but Ernest knew he could take the chap if he had to. After all, a gentleman always protected his lady.

His lady? Well, not quite, although with a little encouragement, he could probably warm to the idea. After all, she was a looker, pretty as a newborn calf and sweeter than his mama's chocolate pecan pie. She was a mite younger than him, but it wasn't like he intended to marry her—or anyone else for that matter.

"I can take care of myself, you know."

What?

"Yes, well," Ernest said slowly, "I suppose you probably can." Out of the corner of his eye, he saw the rogue watching them through the plate-glass window. "So why don't I just leave you and that dandy in there be and head on back to Latanier by myself? I'm sure the two of you can find plenty to talk about on that long ride."

Ernest straightened his cap and waited for her to protest. Instead, the woman had the audacity to look less than pleased at his gallantry.

That did it.

If Genevieve Lamont wanted to ride a hot, dusty bus back to Latanier with that fellow, then she was welcome to it. After all, there were a half dozen other girls who would like to go for a ride in the roadster.

Well, one or two that he knew of, anyway.

"Miss Lamont it's been a real pleasure." He gave his cap one more adjustment then turned to face the irritating woman. "Give your mama my best, and tell your papa I aim to come by and see him soon. I always did intend to find out how he managed to catch three times the fish with the same worms I use."

Head held high, he turned and closed the distance to his car, then lifted his leg over and jumped inside. Before he could crank the engine, Genevieve Lamont caught his attention. In a swirl of skirts, she crossed the road and headed in his direction.

Ernest swiveled to face her, trying hard not to smile. "Change your mind?"

She arrived at the car, face flushed. Her dark eyes peered down at him, her expression surprisingly intense. "Did you know my daddy?"

"Sure." He shrugged. "My brothers and I went fishing with him and my papa off and on all through my growing-up years. Some of my best stories about the one that got away came from him." Ernest gave her a sideways look. "Why?"

Small fingers with perfectly shaped nails drummed a furious rhythm against the door. If it were anyone else touching the roadster, Ernest would have had a fit. Somehow, he didn't mind quite so much when the hand in question belonged to such a pretty thing.

" 'Cause I wonder why you would bring him up now," she said. "How long have you been gone from Latanier?"

"Guess I've been on my own near to four years and worked at the sawmill the last three of those. I try to visit regular, but I haven't seen the folks since Christmas. Been busy trying to get this motorcar running right."

"So you haven't been to Latanier in nearly three months?"

He shook his head. "No. Why do you ask?"

"I just wondered, that's all." She looked away and seemed to be thinking hard on something. When she turned her attention back to him, she looked almost sad. "Did he ever mention me—my daddy, I mean?"

"I don't know. Guess I didn't pay much attention." He shrugged. "He and Papa did all the jawing. The boys and I just fished." A thought occurred. "You know, the last time we all went out in the pirogue he did say something about you."

Her interest piqued. "What did he say?"

"Well, now, let me think." Ernest let that memory play out in his head before he relayed it to the Lamont woman. "Must have been nigh on a year ago. We were fishing in the Fourth of July Chamber of Commerce Fishing Rodeo over in Nouvelle. I took off from work so Papa and your daddy and I could fish together. When Mr. Lamont reeled that big old fish up, I specifically recall him saying how he sure wished his little girl was there to see what he caught."

She looked surprised. "Are you sure about that? Did he mention me by name?"

"Well, no, but do you have a sister?"

Miss Lamont shook her head. "I'm an only child."

"Then he was talking about you."

"But why?"

What a strange woman. "I don't know. It was a record setter, for sure. Maybe he hated it that you missed him winning that five-dollar prize."

"Is that all he said?"

Ernest tried to think, but the memory was fuzzy. "I believe so. He might have said more, but I couldn't say for sure."

Before he could blink, Genevieve Lamont sat beside him, the beat-up cardboard suitcase balanced on her knees. She opened the latch and pulled out a red scarf, then tied it around her hair. That accomplished, she stared straight ahead, saying nothing.

He gripped the steering wheel and tried to make sense of the woman seated beside him. It didn't take him long to figure out not much about her made sense.

"Guess that means we're leaving now," he said.

"Guess so." She held tight to the suitcase and continued to look through the windshield rather than at him.

"Guess so," Ernest repeated as he cranked the engine and slipped the roadster into gear.

They drove four miles in silence, then another half mile with Ernest whistling. Then he heard it; a ping where there should have been a purr. At the curve on Bayou Road, Ernest pulled over under the limbs of an oak tree.

As the motor fell silent, Genevieve Lamont finally turned to look at him, eyes wide. "What's wrong?"

"Probably nothing. I just don't like how she's sounding." Ernest straightened his cap and leapt out of the roadster. "You sit tight. I won't be a minute."

He lifted the hood and tinkered with a wire that looked loose. Satisfied, he slammed the hood shut and slipped behind the wheel. The roadster roared to life, and Ernest threw it into gear.

"You like to work on cars."

It was a statement rather than a question, and it took Ernest by surprise. He glanced over at Miss Lamont, who now sat with her hands in her lap and her suitcase at her feet.

"Yes."

Given the lack of conversation between them until now, Ernest figured he'd heard the last of Genevieve Lamont. After all, another half hour and they'd reach the city limits of Latanier.

"Who taught you?"

Ernest leaned toward her, his gaze fixed on the road ahead. "Who taught me what?"

"Who taught you how to work on cars?"

"Oh." He glanced her way and caught her staring at him. "Guess I picked it up here and there. My papa's handy with things, so I grew up tinkering with this and that. When I first left home, I worked for a man who had an old tractor. He hired me to run that tractor, and I didn't get paid 'lessen I got my work done. When the tractor wouldn't go, I didn't eat. Didn't take me long to figure out how to keep that old John Deere running so my belly wouldn't be empty."

She had the nicest laugh. It struck him that they'd been in each other's company almost an hour, counting Mulotte's Corner Grocery and the bus station, and this was the first time he'd heard it. *I wonder what makes her so sad.*

Up ahead, the familiar landmark indicating the entrance into Latanier loomed. Ernest let off the gas and slowed the roadster a bit. No sense hurrying to get her home when she'd finally started warming up to him.

"How about you and me take a drive before I drop you at home?" He couldn't miss her stricken look. "Or I could come by later on. I bet your daddy would love to take a spin in this little beauty."

"Thank you but no. Mother's not herself." She met his gaze,

and he could have sworn her lower lip trembled a bit. "And Daddy died New Year's Day."

Ernest pressed the accelerator and gripped the wheel. "I'm sorry," was all he could come up with. How had he been gone so long from home that he'd missed hearing about Mr. Lamont's death? And what else had he missed? Maybe he should have read Mama's letters more closely instead of scanning the first line or two then putting them away.

"Just drop me off up there," she said.

His gaze followed the direction in which she pointed. "But that's nearly a quarter mile from your house, Miss Lamont. I don't believe you need to walk that far." He eased the car into a right-hand turn and started up the long driveway to the Lamont homestead. "I'll just head on toward the house and—"

"No!"

Ernest stomped on the brake pedal and nearly sent both of them through the windshield. When the roadster's tires ground to a halt, he shifted into neutral. Before he could say anything, the Lamont woman had her suitcase and her feet on the ground.

"Thank you so much for the ride. Please give my best to your mama and papa." She set off toward the white frame house in the distance, the tail of her red scarf lifting and falling as the breeze crossed her path.

For a moment, Ernest thought of following her and insisting he deposit her on her doorstep like a gentleman should do. She wouldn't let him; that much he knew. So he backed the roadster out of the driveway and drove up a few feet, then killed the engine.

He knew the Lamont woman could not see him or the car for the thick trees. Ernest climbed out and began to follow her on foot, dodging from the cover of a stand of oaks to the privacy of the thick weeds that choked out what looked like it had once been a garden. Three mosquito bites and one encounter with a spiderweb later, he'd just about given up shadowing the girl.

Then she did the strangest thing. Rather than turn right

toward the towering two-story home, she made a sharp left and headed out toward the bayou. Ernest inched forward. *Wonder where she's going.*

Another few feet and he could see her again. Unfortunately, his next step landed him knee deep in bayou mud.

As he yanked his foot out, then dug for his shoe, he decided to head home rather than keep to his task. Where the woman went was none of his business. Besides, nothing went on in Latanier that was a secret.

If Genevieve Lamont was up to something, sooner or later he would hear about it.

three

Genevieve rounded the corner, then stopped and listened as the motorcar's engine roared to life then faded into silence. She knew Ernest had been following her. How could she miss him? A head taller than most bayou boys, the lanky fellow stood out like a sore thumb among the trees and brush lining the driveway.

She smiled despite her irritation. It was nice of him to be concerned. Obviously Ernest's mama had raised him to be a gentleman.

Still, it wouldn't do for him to find her here.

Before she knocked, Gen took a second to compose herself. If Big Mama had the slightest inkling that she was tired or hungry, she'd be bundled off to a hot bath then fed gumbo until she couldn't move.

Not that either of those things wouldn't be heavenly.

"Genevieve, is that you, hon?"

Gen forced the corners of her mouth into a smile and climbed the steps to pull open the screen door. Big Mama met her, took the suitcase, and set it down. Welcoming arms enveloped Gen in a hug.

"Honey, if you're not a sight for sore eyes." She stepped back and put her hands on ample hips. "What you doin' home so early? That bus ain't s'posed to be here for another half hour."

"How is she?" Gen ducked around Big Mama and headed for the back room. "It seems like forever and a day, and I can't hardly stand it."

"Shush now, she's as fine and pretty as ever, but I'd appreciate you letting her sleep just a touch longer before you go waking her up." She touched Gen's arm. "Now answer my question, Genny-girl. How you got home so fast from town?"

Gen reached for her suitcase. "I didn't ride the bus," she said as she opened the latch and reached for the bag from Mulotte's. "I brought you something."

"Who you rode with? Was it a man?"

"Look," Gen said, "cracklings. Your favorite."

Big Mama stared at the bag in Gen's hand then looked directly at Gen. "Don't you try and change the subject, Genny-girl. I asked you a question, and I'll have your hide if'n you don't answer me."

Setting the bag on the table, Gen shrugged. "It was nobody."

"That nobody got a name, or did his mama just name him Nobody cause she thought it was purty?"

Gen pulled one of the mismatched wooden chairs away from the table and sat down. "No," she finally said. "His name is Ernest, Ernest Breaux." She narrowed her eyes and shook her finger at Big Mama. "And don't you dare start making something of nothing. Ernest and I happened to run into each other at the corner grocery. He saw me later at the bus station and offered me a ride. He was going home anyway, so it's not like he made a special trip. I think he was keen on showing his papa his new black motorcar. It's a beauty."

Big Mama stared a moment longer then settled across the table from Gen. "My, my, now that was a lot of words just to say you rode with the neighbor's boy."

"Well, then," Gen said. "Let's just start over." She paused to remove her scarf and set it on the table. "Big Mama, I rode home with Ernest Breaux. You know him. He's the neighbor's boy."

They stared across the table in silence. Gen folded the scarf into a neat triangle, all the while searching her thoughts for something else to say, something to change the conversation from the direction it was going. At this rate Big Mama would have her and Ernest married before summer—in her mind, anyway.

Before Gen could come up with another topic, Big Mama began to giggle. Her giggle turned into a laugh, and before long, Gen couldn't help but join her.

"You always was a sassy thing," Big Mama said.

"I got it from you," Gen replied.

"You did not. You got it all by yourself. Couldn't nobody tell you nothing. Still can't." Big Mama stretched out a dark, gnarled hand, and Gen grasped it. "Genny-girl, I don't know what to do with you sometimes."

Gen entwined her fingers with the larger ones belonging to the woman who helped raise her. "Just love me," she said. "That's about all anyone can do."

Once again Big Mama chuckled. "You're easy to love, hon."

"Not everyone thinks so." Gen released Big Mama's hand and sat back, curling her arms around her middle. "How is she?"

"Your mama's 'bout as well as can be expected." She paused to worry with the corner of her apron. "I 'spect she won't ever get over losing your papa."

"I suppose so." Gen slipped off her right shoe and let the folded bill drop onto the table. "Look what I've got," she said.

Big Mama unfolded the bill. "Five dollars. Where'd you get that kind of money?"

"Betty. She gave it to me and wouldn't take no for an answer when I tried to give it back."

"Well, now," Big Mama said. "Looks like the Lord done provided for your mama's medicines with just enough left over to make two pies."

"Two pies?"

"One for us and one for you to take to that precious Betty. The Lord done smiled on us, and we ought to thank the one who sent the smile. That's the way I see it anyway." She leaned toward Gen. "Does she know?"

Gen shook her head. "No one does."

"Then why'd she up and give you a week's salary?"

"I think she suspects." Gen slipped her foot back into her shoe. "And she's seen my locket."

"Well, whatever the reason, praise the Lord she did it, 'cause I didn't know what I was gonna tell that druggist come

Monday morning." Big Mama pressed both palms on the table and stood. "I ought to be ashamed. I've had a pot of gumbo simmering up at the big house all afternoon. I bet you're starved, and here I ain't even bothered to think about feedin' you."

"Shrimp gumbo?"

Big Mama nodded. "Yes, ma'am. You still like it, don't you?"

"Well, of course I do. Why wouldn't I?"

" 'Cause you're gettin' so skinny and citified that I don't know if my old gumbo's gonna be fit for you. You don't look like you eat nothin', Genevieve Lamont. Am I gonna have to take in your dresses again? That one there's hanging on you like a feed sack."

A familiar sound chased away any statement she might make to the contrary. "Big Mama, do you hear that?"

"I do," she said. "Sounds like a car, it does."

Gen threw open the screen door and headed around the corner to where the path led toward the driveway. Just as she cleared the thicket she saw a motorcar approaching. A black motorcar.

"Land sakes," Big Mama called. "Is that your young man?"

"He's not my young man," she replied. "Why don't you head on up to the house and heat the rice while I see what he wants?"

Thankfully, Big Mama did not argue. She did cast a long look down the driveway before disappearing into the big house.

As the car ground to a stop a few feet away, Gen tried to think of the best way to get rid of its owner. Saying nothing on the ride home hadn't dampened the man's enthusiasm, and she doubted him to be the type to listen to argument either. No, the best thing to do was to act neighborly, then scoot out into the house the first chance she got.

Of course, she'd have to make sure he didn't follow her. Imagine what his reaction would be to Mother and, worse, to the situation with Big Mama, and well. . .she just wouldn't think on it.

"Welcome back," was all she could think to say, and she tried to speak the words without too much enthusiasm. "Forget something?"

"No, but you did."

The Breaux fellow climbed out of the roadster and headed in her direction. Dangling from his outstretched hand was something small and dark.

Her purse.

It must have fallen to the floor when Ernest stopped the car. How could she have forgotten it?

You were in too big a hurry to get home, that's how.

Gen released the breath she hadn't realized she'd been holding and met him halfway. My, but he was tall—and handsome, too, if a girl were to notice things like dreamy brown eyes and coal black hair.

Too bad she didn't have the time or the interest. She might have actually thought him handsome. . .and interesting. . .and maybe even nice.

All right, so he was nice.

"Thank you," she said as grasped the purse and clutched it to her chest. "I'm sorry you had to come all the way back out here."

Ernest shrugged. "Better I return it now than explain to my whole family how a lady's handbag ended up on the floor of my car. Even though you and I know I just offered you a ride home to be neighborly, I'd never hear the end of it." He looked past her to the house. "Everything all right, Miss Lamont?"

Gen followed his gaze and thought she saw someone step away from the upstairs window. Mother's window. No telling what he saw. Mother had taken to wearing Father's pajama's all the time, and she let her waist-length hair hang loose. Poor Ernest probably thought he saw a ghost. Not that she believed in such foolishness.

"Everything's fine," she said. The smell of shrimp gumbo hung heavy in the air, and she thought she heard the screen door groan. *Please don't let Big Mama come out and invite him to supper.*

Ernest gave her a sideways look as he straightened his cap. "You sure?"

"Of course I'm sure."

He didn't look convinced. To his credit, he offered a smile. "Well, then, I'll just be going on home. My best to your mama, and if it wouldn't cause her any upset, would you offer my condolences on your papa's passing?"

"Yes, I'll do that," she said. "I'm sure she would appreciate your saying so."

"How about I come get you Sunday afternoon late, and we take the ride back to New Iberia together? Say around three or four?"

Panic struck her. The last thing she wanted was to ride the bus back to New Iberia, yet spending more time with Ernest Breaux frightened her. With a little encouragement on his part, Gen might start thinking of the handsome fellow as a friend. And after friendship, then what?

"Thank you, but no," she said.

"You sure?"

"Yes, but thank you."

"Well, all right then." Ernest nodded and turned to climb back into the black car. As he pointed the vehicle back toward the main road, he lifted his cap and smiled. "You have a good weekend, Miss Lamont, you hear?"

"Now isn't that nice, him calling you Miss Lamont and all? Shows he's been raised up proper. But then, those Breauxs, they were always good people."

Gen turned around to see Big Mama standing in the shadows behind the screen door. "How much of that did you hear?"

"All of it," she said as she opened the door. "Now come on in here and have some supper."

Though her stomach growled, Gen shook her head. "I can't stand it any longer. You go ahead and fill the bowls," she said as she headed toward Big Mama's house.

"I will, and then I'm gonna draw you a bath, too, you hear?

A good hot one with some of those sweet-smellin' salts you like so much. How does that sound?"

"Like I've died and gone to heaven, Big Mama." As soon as she said the words, Gen wished she could reel them back in. Out of the corner of her eye she saw Mother standing in the upstairs window. "Mother, I'm sorry, I didn't mean to bring up. . .that is, what I meant was just saying that it would feel good to. . ."

Before she could find the words to finish her sentence, Mother was gone.

Gen stumbled toward Big Mama's house, tears stinging her eyes. How careless of her to mention anything about death within earshot of the house. One never knew where Mother was and what she might overhear. Big Mama said that the mention of someone passing would send Mother to bed for days.

Well, she'd gone and done it then. Likening a hot bath to a trip to heaven. "You're an idiot, Genevieve Lamont, a complete idiot."

She sat in the last rays of the April sun, wishing, hoping, praying, and thinking. When the air began to turn cool and the chill swept past, she stood and headed inside.

Unlike the kitchen at the big house, Big Mama's was small and plain. Wooden utensils lay in a wooden bowl and a butcher block held three knives. A bent pot with a mismatched lid sat on the counter next to a stack of fresh-cut greens. Like as not, Big Mama planned on cooking up a mess of them for lunch tomorrow.

Gen ran her hand over the scarred wooden surface of the single cabinet. How many happy childhood hours had she spent playing at Big Mama's feet in this very room? Too many to count, for sure.

She sat cross-legged in the corner and tried to remember what it had been like when Henry, Big Mama's husband, was alive. Funny, while she could remember every detail of most things, she could remember nothing of her father's foreman beyond heavy footsteps on the front porch and big muddy boots left by the screen door.

Oh, but she remembered the day he didn't come home, the day Big Mama stood at the kitchen window and watched Daddy and the sheriff come up the walk. Gen had been too little to understand words like *murder* and *lynching* back then, but she understood them now.

How Big Mama carried on was a mystery, and yet from that terrible day until now, she never failed to believe the Lord had nothing but His best for her. If only Gen could give the Lord that measure of faith.

Of course, Big Mama would say she could.

But then, Big Mama hadn't walked away from God, not even when He allowed her precious Henry to be taken in the most unjust way imaginable. It had taken much less of a calamity to cause Gen to wander from the Lord. No, she turned her back on everything she knew to be good and right for the love of a man.

Love.

Gen chuckled bitterly. What she thought was love turned out to be anything but, and she still bore the scars to prove it.

Inside and out.

"Why didn't You stop me?" she cried into the silence. "You knew everything that would happen and all the people who would be hurt, yet You let me do it anyway."

Bitter tears burned, and she choked them back. God hadn't abandoned her. It had been she who had done the abandoning, choosing her own way over His and Alton Gallier over whatever fellow the Lord had for her.

"Well, whoever you are, I hope you found some nice girl to take my place," she whispered. "I'm not fit for you now."

A sound, soft as the mew of a kitten, caught Gen's attention, and she smiled. In spite of her rebellious choices, the Lord had shown His forgiveness and grace in the most incredible way. Only the heavenly Father could have created such a precious blessing out of such a terrible disaster.

Gen climbed up and steadied herself on the edge of the cabinet, stealing Big Mama's dish towel to wipe her eyes.

"Coming, sweetheart," she called as she headed toward the back bedroom where Ellen Grace Gallier, her four-month-old daughter, lay awake.

four

Ernest slowed the roadster to a crawl so as not to alert the family of his arrival. As he turned the corner and came into view of the house, he began to honk the horn. Papa spilled out of the house first, followed by twelve-year-old Amalie and the eight-year-old twins, Joseph and John.

"Quoi qui se brasse la-bas?" Papa shouted.

"What's going on? Why, I'll tell you, Papa. Come and look. *Vien ici.*"

Mama came rounding the corner, a spade in one hand and a small bucket in the other. His sister Mathilde's son, Teddy, toddled behind her, dragging a tattered blanket in one hand and a piece of sugar cane in the other.

"Why, Ernest, is that you, *bebe?*" Mama called as she set her gardening equipment on the corner of the porch. "What sort of thing is that you're riding in?"

Ernest set the brake and climbed out to embrace his mother, then kiss the top of her head. "It's a roadster, Mama. A 1927 Model T roadster with a convertible top and a rumble seat." He looked up at his father. "What do you think of her, Papa?"

"Well, now," Papa said slowly, "she's a beauty, eh?"

"Yeah, she's a beauty," little sister Amalie exclaimed. "Can I learn to drive her, Ernest?"

Ernest lifted his sister in the air and whirled her around, then set her down on unsteady feet. "You're twelve years old and a girl, Amalie. What on earth do you want to learn how to drive for?"

"Oh, I don't know," she said in that dreamy way she had. "There could be any number of reasons for me to learn. What if Mama was to need something in town and Papa and the boys weren't here to go fetch it?"

"*Sa fait pas rien*. Then she'd just do without, *cher*, because no girl of mine's gonna go gallivanting about in a motorcar alone." Papa ignored Amalie's frown to run his hand over the back of the seat. "Ernest, how did you manage to pay for this contraption? It must have set you back a pretty penny."

"Not as much as you'd think," Ernest said. "I got a deal on it. My boss was about to sell it for scrap metal because the body had some dings and the motor kept going out. Well, you know how you always taught me to be handy around mechanical things?"

Papa nodded.

"I found out there's not much difference in overhauling a tractor engine and repairing one of these. Here, take a look at this." He flipped the latch and opened the hood. "Isn't that something? See, here's where the problem was."

A short while later, Papa finished his examination of the roadster and was ready for a ride. He climbed inside and settled the twins on his lap while Amalie took a spot in the rumble seat. "Come on and get in, Mama."

"*Mais, non.*" She waved them away with a shake of her hand, then lifted Teddy into her arms. "If the good Lord means me to ride around in one of those things, He'll tell me Himself. You all go ahead and enjoy yourselves, and I'll go back to my Easter lilies. Besides, the babies will be awake soon."

"*Allons*, Mama. Amalie will stay with the *bebes*. Eileen and Mary are four and three. Surely this girl can pull her nose out of her book long enough to take care of them while we go for a ride," he added, ignoring Amalie's outraged cry.

"*Non, merci.* You all go on," she said.

Ernest set out across the yard, circling the barn and the henhouse before turning the roadster toward town. Once he got into Latanier, he had to pull over outside the barbershop so Papa could show his buddies the motorcar.

Of course, they all wanted to look under the hood, and most asked for a ride around the town square as well. Amalie never moved from her seat in the back, but after a few circles, the twins opted to sit and wave as the car went by. Finally, as the sun sunk below the oaks, Ernest headed the car for home.

Out of the corner of his eye, he could see his father watching his every move while holding one sleeping twin on each shoulder. The thought occurred to Ernest that if Mama and Papa hadn't elected to fill their home with young'uns, they might have had some time and money for the finer things in life.

Things like a black 1927 Model T roadster with a convertible top and a rumble seat.

Then and there, Ernest vowed that he would live his life to the fullest, never making the mistake his parents had. To be sure, he didn't mind at all the benefits of coming from a large family. There was always someone to talk to or play with when he was little and always someone to help now that he was older.

The trouble came in feeding all those mouths and seeing to their health and education. Why, they nearly lost little Amalie to the fever back in '29, and just this past winter, the whole bunch of them came down with the dreaded influenza. If his brother-in-law the doctor hadn't treated the family for free, Papa would've had to take a second job just to pay the bill.

It was too much to consider, this burden a wife and children put on a man. To his way of thinking, any blessing they might bring was not worth the cost.

From this moment on, Ernest Breaux determined he would be a confirmed bachelor, never to be called Husband or Papa. No, the roles of big brother and uncle fit him just fine. That way he could enjoy the little ones, then send them back to their mamas when they went to fussing.

To his mind, a perfect arrangement.

He made one more circle around the house, then pulled up next to the porch and took one of the twins from Papa. The little fellow opened his eyes, then closed them again and snuggled against Ernest's shirt.

"Ernest, you have a way with the babies," Mama said. "You should have a houseful, you know."

He smoothed Joseph's hair and lifted him into his mother's arms. At eight, the child's legs nearly touched the ground when Mama held him, yet he slept soundly. "No babies for me. You'll have to get your grandchildren from the others."

"Oh, you'll change your mind soon enough." Mama shifted Joseph to the other shoulder. "Just you wait and see. When you meet the right girl, well, that's all it will take. *C'est tout.*"

"It's not going to happen, Mama. Even if I do meet the right girl, I'm too old to start a family," he said as he climbed out of the roadster to join the rest of the family at the supper table. "I'm nigh on to thirty and far too set in my ways to change them now."

"You're no older than your papa was when I met him." Mama strolled past Papa and patted him on the arm. "Tell your son he's not too old to have a passel of young'uns, Theo."

Rather than respond, Papa chuckled and gave Mama a kiss on the cheek. He whispered something in Mama's ear that set her bustling off to the kitchen with a blush on her cheeks.

As Ernest settled into his spot beside Papa, he cast a glance around the table. Between siblings, nieces, and nephews, the big table was full, and another had been fashioned from a piece of wood and a barrel to hold the overflow.

He'd have to make something more suitable when he got a chance. His boss down at the sawmill had told him he could have his pick of the scrap lumber if he ever wanted to build something. Maybe now was the time to take him up on his offer. Ernest could fix a decent table and some chairs that the little ones would fit in. What with his sisters Angeline and Mathilde having babies like they were going out of style, it looked as though there would be a continual need for places to seat the children.

Little Joseph climbed off his stool at the makeshift table and tugged on Ernest's shirttail. "I wanna sit with you, Ernest."

"All right," Ernest replied as he hefted the youngster onto his left knee. "But you're not gonna get my chicken leg, you hear?"

Teddy raised a wail from his place in Mama's lap. "Me, too," he cried. "Me sit wit Unka Ernie."

Joseph's twin, John, stood and headed Ernest's way. "If Joe's gonna sit there, I'm gonna, too."

Four-year-old Eileen and her shadow, three-year-old Mary, scrambled to join the group. "Mary and me, too," she said, speaking for her sister as she always did.

Ernest looked down at the youngest Breaux. "You, too, Mary?"

The little girl nodded. She rarely spoke. She didn't have to, as Eileen rarely left her side.

"C'est tout," Papa said. "We will all sit in our own places and leave Ernest in peace to eat his dinner, eh?" He leaned toward Ernest. "You're like the Pied Piper in that nursery rhyme, son. All the little ones, they want to follow you wherever they go, eh?"

Ernest shrugged. "I hadn't noticed."

"Well, you should. Don't think it has missed the Lord's attention, even if it missed yours."

"You're as bad as Mama," he said with a grin. "And I'll tell you what I told her. You're going to have to get your grandbabies from the others. This fellow's got plans, and they don't include bottles and diapers. *Le jeu vaut pas la chandelle.*"

"Oh, you think it's not worth it? Well, we will see, won't we? You can make all the plans you want, son, but it's the heavenly Father who decides, not you, eh?" Papa waited until the twins returned to the little table, then raised his hand to silence the chatter. "Gather your hands, and let's thank *le bon Dieu* for this food," he said, and then he spoke a blessing over the meal.

Thankfully, the dinner conversation stayed away from the topic of babies. Instead, Papa questioned him endlessly about the mechanics of the roadster's engine and the technique of driving the vehicle.

Finally, as Mama and the girls disappeared into the kitchen, Ernest and Papa headed for the front porch. Settling into a chair beside his father in the fading twilight, Ernest closed his eyes and thanked God for placing him here. With the crickets chirping a bayou symphony, a deep contentment settled into Ernest's bones. The only thing that felt better than sitting right here was driving the roadster through New Iberia.

"How about I show you how tomorrow? You're a natural." He snapped his fingers. "I know you'd pick it up just like that."

Papa shook his head. "Mais non, son. I've too much work to be playing at driving a motorcar."

Ernest pushed back from the table and reached for his coffee cup. "Like what?"

His father ticked off a list of a half-dozen chores that needed doing and three errands he planned to run in the pirogue.

"Fine." He took a sip of the strong chicory brew. "So how long you figure the chores will take? Most of the morning?"

"And probably on into the afternoon, son. Why?"

"Because it'll take two men half the time." He smiled. "And those errands you plan to do by boat? Wonder if they might be run just as easily in that roadster out front."

Papa laughed and slapped Ernest on the shoulder. "You know, boy, I believe you just might be on to something. Now if I can just get your mama to stop worrying every time I set foot in a motorcar, eh?"

"What are you menfolk talking about? Did I hear my name?"

"*Oui*, Cleo," Papa said as he gathered Mama onto his lap and kissed her soundly. "I was telling Ernest here how you cannot bear to be apart from me."

Mama's blush combined with her giggle took take two decades off her age. "Theo, you are the worst of rascals, you hear? You were saying no such thing."

"You been eavesdropping on the menfolk, cher? If your uncle Joe were alive, he'd surely send you off to get an earful from your *Tante* Flo." Papa turned to smile at Ernest. "Lord rest their souls, those two put up with more than a body ought to take from this one."

"You hush now, Theophile Breaux. Don't be giving the boy ideas that his mama was trouble."

Papa chuckled and wrapped his arms tighter around Mama.

"You were trouble then and you're trouble still. You're lucky that you're the kind of trouble I like." He nuzzled her neck. "And I still say you were eavesdropping."

Mama climbed out of his lap and shook her head. "It's not eavesdropping when the menfolk are talking loud enough to be heard." She pointed at Ernest. "And you, well, I don't believe you must like my shrimp étouffée much."

"But, Mama, why do you say that? You know it's my favorite."

His mother smoothed the corner of her apron and started down the porch steps. "Because if you teach your papa to drive that motorcar, there will be no étouffée for you at the supper table tomorrow night."

"Aw, Mama." Ernest rose to follow her. "That's not fair. Isn't Papa the head of this household? If he asks me to do something, are you really expecting me to go against him?"

Mama seemed to be giving his question proper thought. Finally she squared her shoulders and looked beyond him to Papa. "Of course not, Ernest. You should always mind your papa."

Ernest gave his father a sideways look and noted the amusement on his face, then turned his attention back to Mama. Her expression was much more serious.

"Of course, I expect your papa not to ask something of you that he shouldn't. Something like teaching him to drive one of those dangerous motorcars." With that, Mama stormed away and disappeared around the side of the house.

Papa leaned over and clapped his hand on Ernest's shoulder. "Don't worry about your mama, son. She's a handful, but she knows I love her, eh? What I would do without her, I can't imagine."

Ernest leaned back against the house and closed his eyes, trying to imagine being a part of a pair like Papa and Mama. Try as he might, he couldn't picture it.

"Why you don't want to get hitched, son?"

Opening his eyes, he regarded his father. "You really want to know?"

Papa nodded.

"You see that car over there?"

Again his father nodded.

"I like driving it. And I like living in town and being foot-loose and fancy-free." He shrugged. "A family man, he can't be like that. He has responsibilities."

"I suppose so." His papa looked thoughtful. "You know, son, you and I are a lot alike."

The statement struck Ernest as odd. Other than their looks, he and his father were nothing alike. Where Papa was content to be a husband, father, and bayou man, Ernest had picked the life of a city fellow, no strings and no cares.

"Would you believe I nearly lost your mother for the very reason you state, eh? I thought seeing the world was what I was meant to do. I never told you this, but I got halfway to Canada before I realized what I was looking for sat back in Joe Trahan's house beside Bayou Nouvelle."

Now this was interesting. Still, he found it impossible to see his father as a rambling man. Theo Breaux was the most loyal, home-loving man Ernest knew.

"Oui, your mama, she was going to teach school. Her uncle Joe—he and Tante Flo, they raised her, you know—well, she had him talked into sending her to that fancy teacher's college over in New Orleans. Had my papa not broke his leg, I would have been off seeing the world and some other fellow would have built your mama a schoolhouse." Papa sighed. "She like to killed me, you know?"

"What?" Ernest chuckled. "Mama? I don't believe it."

"Believe it, son. The first time I met your mama, she caused me to fall through a roof. Or maybe that was the second time. I don't recall clearly. Still, I wore more bruises during our courtship than I've managed to collect in all the years since."

They shared a laugh; then silence fell between them. A question began to plague Ernest, and it wouldn't leave him alone until he asked it out loud. "Papa," he said slowly, "if I ask you something, would you tell me the truth?"

"Oui," Papa said. "If I can, that is."

"All right." He lowered his voice in case Mama was still in the vicinity. "Do you ever regret it? Turning in your traveling shoes for. . ." He paused to consider his words. "For the yoke of a wife and a family."

"No."

"You didn't even take time to think about it."

His father shook his head. "Don't have to. See, I had this very same conversation with my father nigh on thirty years ago. He told me the same thing I'm telling you. What one man looks on as a burden, another sees as a blessing. I'm beholden to le bon Dieu to the blessings He has given me. All of them. And the plans for adventure, well, we can make them, but the Lord, He decides."

"But the adventure you gave up—do you ever wonder what you missed?"

Papa smiled. "Your mama is all the adventure I'll ever need. All of it and then some."

The pair lapsed once more into companionable silence. Finally Papa spoke. "You intend to work at that sawmill all your life?"

"I don't rightly know, Papa. Guess I hadn't given it much thought."

"I see." He closed his eyes. "This sure is a comfortable bench. I believe you made this one, didn't you? And that one you're sitting on, too?"

"I believe so. Why?"

"Next time you're speaking to the Father, you might want to ask Him why He gave you such a talent for making things from scrap wood. You don't seem to be using it."

Now that was an odd statement. Where did that come from? "I'll do that, Papa," Ernest said. "Now about that driving lesson tomorrow."

Papa opened one eye and grinned. "Not necessary."

"Well, that's a relief."

"I already know how to drive. Your brother-in-law the

doctor taught me. In case of emergency, you know?"

"I see."

Papa closed his eyes once more, and this time his grin tilted higher. "Yes, sir, you won't have to teach me a thing, except how to start that beauty. I can take it from there."

five

Gen watched the Saturday morning sun rise above the trees from her bedroom window. Ellen had spent most of the night in fitful sleep, and thus so had Gen. Still, as the orange glow chased away the night sky, she sat in the little straight-backed chair lost in thought.

She'd climbed out this very window a year and a half ago last week to meet up with Alton Gallier down by the crosses behind the churchyard. From there they eloped, then lit out for Texas and the oil-patch life in Port Neches, where Alton's uncle had secured him a job on the crew working the new Bessie Heights Field.

The little shanty they rented on the edge of town had seemed cozy, at least until the morning sickness came. Not too long after, the walk out back to do her morning necessities turned into a several-times-a-night trip.

By then, Alton had taken to working the night shift, so she made the walk alone, often fighting the swarms of mosquitoes and running from threats both real and imagined. Sometimes Alton was the threat.

Even now the memory of those nights made her shiver.

Had it really been just a year and a half since she left her life here in Latanier? Some days it seemed like a lifetime ago. Gen had certainly done enough living for two lifetimes since then.

When she thought of those days, Gen couldn't help but remember the loneliness. Newly wedded bliss gave way to long hours at work for Alton and long hours alone for Gen.

She missed her family terribly, but Daddy had forbidden her to see Alton Gallier, and Mother said she'd never speak to her again if Gen married up with Alton. Gen figured neither parent wanted to hear from her, leastways not for a while.

Only after she found herself expecting Ellen did she stop to think what Mother and Daddy were going through. When her letters were returned unopened, she wrote Big Mama, who answered promptly.

By then, it was too late. Daddy had taken sick and Mother, well she'd taken to honoring her promise that Gen ceased to exist.

Ellen wasn't a month old when Gen tucked her pride into her back pocket and walked up the dirt road to home, only to find a funeral wreath on the front door. Daddy had passed on not three days before. When she finally found Mother, dressed in Daddy's pajamas and asleep on his side of the bed, she realized she'd lost her mother, too.

Only Big Mama greeted her warmly.

Gen's gaze wandered past the treetops to the spot where Big Mama's cabin stood hidden by the thicket. A plume of smoke told Gen that Big Mama was up and most likely brewing coffee.

She rose to gather a still-sleeping Ellen into her arms. With the baby snuggled in the crook of her arm, Gen settled once more in the chair beside the window.

"You see that smoke, Ellen? That's where God's favorite angel on earth lives."

᠈᠊

"Look at that precious angel," Big Mama said as Gen settled at the table in the little cabin with Ellen in her lap. "I do declare, she's the spitting image of her mama at that age."

"You think so?"

"I sure do." She smiled. "Remember now, I got to see you even before your mama did. That poor thing, she was bone tired from her laborin', and your daddy, he was beside himself with worry. When you finally decided to make your appearance, Miss Rose, she could barely lift an arm to hold you, and Mr. Carl was scared he was gonna drop you."

Gen nodded. As many times as she'd been told the story of her birth, Gen never tired of hearing it.

"I took hold of you, and you looked up and me and smiled. That old doctor, he didn't believe me, but I swear that's the honest truth. It's been you and me ever since, hasn't it?"

"Sure has," she said.

Big Mama spoke the truth. Gen never tired of sitting at Big Mama's feet or, better yet, in her lap, as her mother's housekeeper did her chores or cooked the evening meal. Funny how her memories of Mother paled in comparison to thoughts of Big Mama.

Mother used to joke that Gen didn't know which of them was her mother until she got old enough to notice the difference between Mother's light skin and fair hair and Big Mama's dark African features.

Ellen peered up at Gen with wide eyes. "I wonder if she knows who I am."

"Of course she does." Big Mama set a mug of steaming coffee in front of Gen, then took her own mug and settled across from her. "A baby knows its mama."

"I didn't. Mother told me so."

She looked surprised. "Well, that's different. Your mama's health, it was delicate, you know. Still is, for that matter. I just stepped in and helped her however I could. That was nothing like this here with Ellen. Look at that child; she loves you. It's plain as day."

Gen shook her head. "She's just a baby, and her mama's not the one taking care of her."

Big Mama waved away the statement with a lift of her hand. "That's just temporary. But that baby knowing her mama, well, that's something God makes sure of. Why wouldn't He do that when a mama loves her baby as much as you do?"

Before Gen could respond, Big Mama answered her own question.

"He's a good and merciful God, that's why." She paused to shake her head. "He knew all of this would happen before you and that baby's daddy were ever born." Big Mama took a sip of coffee and sighed. "He knew everything in the past, and He knows what's gonna happen in the future."

"I suppose."

"Ain't no supposin' to it. He said it, I believe it, and that's that."

Gen considered Big Mama's simple way of thinking. If only she could have such faith. She shifted Ellen to her shoulder. "Do you ever wonder why?"

Big Mama leaned back in the chair and gave her a sideways look. "What do you mean?"

"I mean, do you ever wonder why things happen? Why God lets people do things He knows will hurt them?" Gen smoothed Ellen's dark hair, already curly and unruly even at her young age. "I guess what I'm asking is, if He loves me so much, why didn't He stop me when He saw me about to do something so. . ." Her voice betrayed her, and she bit her lip until the moment passed. "Something so hurtful."

"Well now," Big Mama said, "you done asked the question of the ages, Genny-girl. The Lord, He don't have to tell nobody why. They's a few things I'd like Him to explain, too."

"Like what happened to Henry."

She nodded her dark head then looked past Gen. "That's part of it."

"What else?"

Big Mama shook her head. "I done said enough. Now why don't we talk about something pleasant? Like maybe that young man who carried you home from New Iberia yesterday. He looked like he might be one of the Breaux boys."

"Yes, he's a Breaux." Gen kissed Ellen on the top of her head then smoothed her dark hair. "Ernest. The eldest. Don't you remember? I told you that already."

"I 'spect you did, now that I'm thinking on it." Big Mama's eyes narrowed. "That boy sweet on you?"

"Sweet? No. Why, I hardly know him."

"It don't take much knowin' to set a fellow to chasin' a pretty girl." She reached for the teaspoon and jabbed it into the sugar bowl. "You been keeping time with him?"

"No, ma'am," she said. "I only ran into him at the corner grocery yesterday."

Teaspoon poised above her coffee cup, Big Mama tilted it to allow the sugar to sprinkle into the cup. "Then how came he to offer to tote you home?"

"He was being a gentleman, I suppose." She pushed back from the table and stood. "Why all the questions, Big Mama? He's not interested in me, and I'm not interested in him, so that's that. Besides, you and I both know I'm a married woman."

"I do know that, and I pray ever night for the Lord to either bring Alton Gallier back to walking with Him or take him home to glory." She shrugged. "Either way's all right with me."

Gen didn't dare think about which of those choices she would prefer. Her opinions of Alton Gallier were still colored by feelings she had barely begun to learn to live with.

Or in her husband's case, live without.

Ellen stirred and began to make whimpering sounds. Gen lulled her back to sleep by settling into the old rocker by the fireplace.

"So he just up and asked you to ride in that fancy car 'cause he happened to see you at the corner grocery?" She frowned. "Do I look like I just fell off the turnip truck? There's more to that story than that."

"All right." Gen lowered her voice. "There was a rough character in line ahead of me at the bus station. Mr. Breaux happened to see that he was making familiar conversation with me, and he rescued me from the situation." She paused. "Did you know he used to go fishing with Daddy?"

"That I did. He and his brothers used to head out with Mr. Carl and Mr. Theo Breaux. Me and your mama would pack them a mess of food in a pail, and they'd fish until suppertime." Big Mama rose to clear the table. "You know his mama always brings us an Easter lily from her garden come spring, and the pecan pies she makes, well, I do declare I'd love to be a fly on her kitchen wall so's I could see what she puts in her pecan pie that makes it so good."

Gen shook her head. "Why don't you just ask her?"

The moment she said the words, she wanted to reel them back in. Giving Big Mama an excuse to visit the Breaux place would be a recipe for disaster, not for pecan pie.

"Or maybe I could find out for you." She paused to try and pass an innocent look by Big Mama. "You never know when I'll see Ernest Breaux again."

"Well, that's right," Big Mama said. "You just don't ever know."

six

"You going to let that young man tote you back to town?"

Gen straightened her back and stabbed at the ground with her hoe. Rather than endure silent hours in Mother's home, she'd elected to spend Saturday afternoon trying to make the beginnings of a garden from a patch of weeds on the south side of the house.

Daddy swore this section of the property bore the biggest tomatoes in Latanier, but so far she'd found nothing left of the prized vines. Before she caught the bus back to town tomorrow afternoon, she was determined to at least uncover what was left of her father's handiwork.

"I asked you a question, Genny-girl. Now don't you go thinkin' just 'cause you're all growed up and a mama now that you can ignore your Big Mama."

Big Mama wore an apron embroidered with apples over her Sunday-go-to-meeting dress. Gen smiled.

"Why are you all dressed up on a Saturday afternoon?"

"Ellen, she's down for her nap, and your mama's sleepin', too. I aim to go a-visitin'," she said with her I-dare-you-to-argue look.

Visiting? Oh, no.

Unless she missed her guess, there were probably two or three pecan pies cooling in the kitchen. As sure as she stood there, Gen knew Big Mama would make a beeline for the Breaux place with one of them as soon as she tore off her apron and slipped into her church shoes.

Gen knocked the dirt off the knees of Daddy's overalls and shook her head. "Big Mama, please don't."

"Don't what?" Her sassy look turned sweet and innocent as she rested her hands on her ample hips. "Can't a body be neighborly anymore?"

"Not when it's just a poor excuse for meddling."

Big Mama had the decency to look offended. "Well, I don't know where you think I'm headed, but I've got a mess of fish all fried up and a pot of red beans dished out and ready to go next door."

"Next door?"

"Yes'm. The Widow LeBlanc's been feeling a mite poorly lately." She paused. "And on top of that, I thought if I brought her some vittles she just might share that squash casserole recipe she brought to church last time they had dinner on the grounds. If I don't get it soon, she's gonna head off to Mississippi to live with her daughter, and I'll never know what she puts in it."

"The Widow LeBlanc?" Gen looked past Big Mama to the brilliant blue sky and tufts of white cotton-ball clouds. Even seen slightly blurry because of her poor distance vision, it was beautiful.

"Who did you think I was headin' t'see?" She smiled. "Oh, you thought your Big Mama was goin' t'meddle in your love life?"

She shrugged. "I hardly know the man. It's not even a friendship."

Big Mama put on her sternest expression. "Well, as long as you're a married woman, there ain't gonna be no other man in your life. The good Lord, He will be what your man can't—or won't. The Bible, it says so. I done read that t'you many times."

"Yes, ma'am," she said as she yanked the hoe out of the dirt. "And I'm perfectly happy with the Lord as my husband."

Indeed she was. True, the situation wasn't what she'd expected when she had hightailed it out of Latanier to elope with Alton Gallier, but things could be worse.

Big Mama whirled around and headed back to the kitchen, only to return a few minutes later with a plate wrapped in a dish towel and a black iron pot dangling from the crook of her arm. "I won't be long," she said as she adjusted the dish towel.

"I'll stay close and listen for Ellen and Mother."

"All right then," she said, although she made no move to leave. Finally she shook her head. "You didn't answer me."

"I didn't? What did you ask?"

"I asked you if that Breaux feller was coming tomorrow to carry you back to town in that motorcar of his."

"No," she said. "I'll be catching the bus at three o'clock like always."

Big Mama frowned. "You mean to tell me that rascal didn't even offer to fetch you?"

"Yes, ma'am," she said. "He asked. I told him no, thank you."

The older woman studied her for a moment then nodded. "Smart girl. Men like that, they are pretty on the eyes and hard on the heart. You done got enough trouble without taking up with the likes of him."

Gen chuckled and went back to work, stopping only when thirst drove her inside for some of Big Mama's sweet tea. A few minutes after two, Ellen's cry echoed across the yard, and Gen raced inside to fetch the baby from her crib.

She tiptoed past Mother's closed door, tempted for the briefest moment to stop and listen for sounds of life inside. What Mother did all day behind that door puzzled Gen, and she wondered if her solitude was because Gen was home.

When Big Mama returned, she would ask. Maybe Mother only hid from her and not from the rest of the world.

After a feeding and a diaper change, Ellen was content to lie on a freshly starched blanket on the grass. As Gen struggled with the weeds and clumps of hard dirt, she watched her little girl.

Someday Ellen would be all grown up. What would she tell Ellen about her papa?

Out of the corner of her eye, a flash of white caught her attention. She looked up to see Mother standing half-hidden in the shadows of her open bedroom window. Dressed in a pair of Daddy's pajamas with her hair captured in a thick braid that hung over her right shoulder, Gen's once-beautiful mother looked more like one of those ghosts from the scary tales the bayou boys told.

"Mother, why don't you come down here and sit a spell?"

Rather than respond, her mother slipped back into the shadows, leaving darkness where she once stood.

"Genny-girl, come quick."

Gen whirled around to see Big Mama hustling up the drive, waving something white. As she neared, Gen could make out a piece of paper in Big Mama's hand. The look on her face told Gen that Big Mama had returned from the Widow LeBlanc's house with more than just a recipe for squash casserole.

Ellen had begun to fuss again, so she scooped the baby into her arms. "What is it?"

"That fool mailman, he done dropped off a letter to the Widow LeBlanc that ought to have been delivered here. A letter for you."

"For me?"

"That's right."

Gen traded Ellen for the letter then studied the envelope. There was no return address, but since the postmark read Beaumont, Texas, it could only be from one person.

Her husband.

Big Mama expelled a long breath and shook her head. "Open it, Genevieve. That letter's not gonna open itself."

Gen sank onto the grass and held the letter to her chest. "I don't want to."

"Then I will," Big Mama said. She handed Ellen to Gen, took the envelope, and tore it open. A letter folded in half and written longhand fluttered to the ground. Gen reached to hand it back to Big Mama, then kissed the top of Ellen's head.

As her gaze scanned the page, Big Mama's eyes widened. "Land o' Goshen," she said when she finished. "I swan, I don't believe what I just read."

Gen clutched Ellen so tight the baby wailed a complaint. "What is it?" she asked as she soothed the infant.

Big Mama settled on the grass beside her, obviously ignoring the fact that her best dress would need a good cleaning when she stood. "Genny-girl, I don't know how to tell you this. It ain't from Alton, but it sure is about him."

A half-dozen thoughts danced across her mind. He might be in jail, or in the hospital, or maybe he'd filled another woman's head with empty promises and run off with her.

"Just read it."

Nodding, Big Mama cleared her throat and began to read. Words like *accident* and *job site* and *fatal* combined with phrases like *our most sincere condolences* and *with deepest sympathy* to send a buzz through her ears and jolt her heart. A final sentence said something about insurance and how a representative would contact the widow shortly.

The widow.

Gen had barely begun to get used to being a wife when she became a mother. Now she would have to learn how to be a widow.

She waited to feel something. Sadness, anger, loss—anything. She felt nothing. It was as if a door had slammed shut somewhere off in the distance, and she'd been told about it but hadn't actually heard the sound.

And then the exhaustion arrived. Wave upon wave hit her, crumpling her into a ball. She lay on the blanket and tucked Ellen beside her, then stared up at the brilliant blue sky. All the clouds had danced away except one. It hung directly above her.

In that moment, she knew the day she had been dreading, the day Alton Gallier blew back into her life, would never come. The Lord would indeed be her husband now, and little Ellen's papa, too.

Tired.

So tired.

Ellen closed her eyes and Gen followed suit. Ashamed at her relief, she felt tears sting her eyes. "I'm sorry I wished him dead, Big Mama. That was just awful of me."

"Hush now," Big Mama said. "You loved that boy best as you could, and you'd of kept on loving him had he been the husband and father the Lord called him to be."

"But I never wanted it to be like this. I only. . ."

Words fell away and left her speechless.

"Oh, honey." Big Mama wrapped her strong arms around Gen and Ellen. "You don't have to be afraid of Alton Gallier no more, that's for sure."

Somehow Gen managed to nod.

"And come the day that insurance check arrives, your Alton, he will have done one last good thing for his wife and daughter."

Gen lifted her head. "What do you mean?"

"Look here." Big Mama pointed to the last line of the letter. "See, the company, they're paying a death benefit. It won't make us rich, but it sure will add to what you're making at the five-and-dime."

Gen checked the figure twice, closed her eyes, and offered up a prayer of thanks. Three hundred dollars was a fortune, much more than she could make in six months at the five-and-dime. It wouldn't last forever, but with that nest egg in the bank to cover Mama's medicines and emergencies, she could find a little relief. It would go far in paying for Daddy's funeral expenses, too.

Maybe in a short while, she could even think of working fewer hours or even finding a job closer to home. Not that there were many jobs to be had. The country had been through years of hard times, and she should be thankful she had any work at all. Still, leaving Ellen became harder each time she did it, and eventually she knew she would just flat have to stop.

"Lord, hasten that day," she whispered.

৯

That evening on the bus ride home, she fell into a deep sleep. Awaking as the bus pulled into New Iberia, Gen realized she hadn't slept so well since Ellen's birth; or before actually.

Back in the boardinghouse, she dropped her suitcase and climbed into bed. The next thing she realized, it was Monday morning, and Betty stood over her.

"Awake at last," she said. "I was beginning to get worried about you."

Gen bolted upright and shook her head. She'd been in the middle of the strangest dream. Mother was driving a motorcar that looked strangely like Ernest Breaux's. Her father rode beside Mother with Gen and Ellen in the rumble seat. Running behind them, trying furiously to catch up, was Alton Gallier.

He'd almost reached the car when Betty shook her awake, and the sensation of having her arm grabbed had made her think Alton caught her. She looked up at Betty, and the strangest thing happened.

She began to cry.

Five minutes and two handkerchiefs later, Gen managed to relate the dream to Betty, carefully leaving out any reference to the identities of Ellen or Alton. The less Betty knew about her life, the better. It was shameful enough that she'd defied her parents to run off with a man like Alton, and even more shameful that she'd given birth to a daughter she wasn't raising.

No, better to keep her secrets and let Betty think what she would rather than know the truth.

Her roommate sat very still at the end of the bed. She seemed to be deep in thought. Finally, she gave Gen a direct look. "Something big happened this weekend, didn't it?"

Gen blew her nose and nodded.

"Anything you care to tell me about? I'm a good listener, you know. And what I'm told I keep to myself."

This much was true. She knew Betty to be a good friend and a godly woman. She'd seen firsthand at the five-and-dime how her friend hated gossip.

Oh, no, the five-and-dime. She dropped the handkerchief and threw back the covers. "Oh, Betty, what time is it?"

Betty placed her hand on Gen's shoulder. "Hold on there, kid. There's no need to hurry. I already went down to the five-and-dime and told Lester you weren't feeling yourself." She gave Gen a stern look. "You're not, are you?"

Gen shook her head. "No, I guess I'm not. I've never slept this much or cried this hard, not even when my daddy died. I guess I just bottled it all up inside until that awful dream made it all let loose."

"Looks like you needed to let it loose," Betty said. "A body can't hold that kind of stuff in forever. I do believe the Lord fetches people home in His time, but some days I wish He might be a little slower with the fetching. Why, I don't know what I'd do if I lost my papa. And I think about Dorothy and raising that baby after her husband was killed."

As soon as the words fell from Betty's lips, Gen's tears began to flow again. This time it took more than five minutes and a sizeable corner of the bed sheet to dry her eyes. She blew her nose twice, then fell back onto her pillow, exhausted. As her eyes closed, she waited for sleep to return.

"Oh, no, you don't." Betty yanked off the covers and stood with her hands on her hips. "If I let you go back to sleep, I might never wake you up." She shrugged. "And what good's a roommate who does nothing but sleep?"

Gen reluctantly sat back up. Head aching from the intensity of her crying, she reeled a bit before steeling her backbone to remain upright.

"I'm afraid I'm not going to be good for much today," she said.

"That's not true." Betty offered her a hand, and she took it, rising to stand on unsteady feet. Before Gen could protest, Betty yanked the sheets off Gen's bed, then did the same with her own. "While I go run these down to the Washateria, you make coffee."

By the time Betty returned, Gen had washed her face and combed her hair. She removed the coffeepot from the little electric burner and poured two cups. With the sheets and blankets stripped from their beds, the room looked bare and depressing. Gen felt tears press against her eyelids.

"Oh, no, you don't." Betty sipped at the strong black brew. "No more tears until the sheets are dry."

Gen giggled, although her good humor didn't quite reach her heart.

"You don't have to say a thing if you don't want to." Betty nodded toward the open window. "How about we take this coffee out on the terrace?"

The "terrace" was actually an oversized ledge reached by climbing through the westward-facing window and just big enough for the two of them. On pleasant days, the pair often ended the day here.

Somehow it seemed appropriate to begin one in the familiar place. Especially since things seemed so horribly unfamiliar.

She was a widow.

How awful that she couldn't grieve the loss of her husband as any normal wife would. The truth be known, she'd lost Alton Gallier long before he actually departed this life.

"Warm enough?"

Betty settled beside her and stretched out her legs, then covered them with her winter coat. The air felt fresh with the slightest bite of north wind. Gen huddled close to Betty and sipped at the steaming coffee.

They sat in silence for a bit. Finally Gen set her coffee cup on the ledge and turned to face Betty. Her friend offered a smile.

"You don't have to say a word, you know."

"I know." Gen slid beneath the warmth of Betty's coat. "But I think I need to tell you."

"All right," Betty said.

Gen took a deep breath and let it out slowly. As she touched her fingers to the locket at her neck, the simple heart that held a lock of Ellen's dark hair, she closed her eyes.

"My husband," she said slowly, "is dead. I'm not even twenty-one years old, and I'm a widow."

"Oh, honey," Betty said.

"You don't know the half of it." Gen paused. "He's dead and I'm glad." Tears overtook her. "That's not true," she managed. "I do care, but I'm glad I don't have to be afraid of him anymore. Is that horribly selfish?"

"Oh, Genevieve, no! It isn't horribly selfish." Betty shook

her head. "Remember when we met?"

Gen nodded. "At the bus station?"

"That's right. You were fresh off the bus from Latanier, and I'd just arrived from Crowley. Your bus was early and mine was late, or we'd never have met. If that's not God's timing, I don't know what is."

She attempted a smile. Finding a friend like Betty in a city the size of New Iberia had definitely been a blessing.

"You know, honey, the Lord, He sets the lonely in families." She shrugged. "Since neither of us has anyone in New Iberia, I figure the Lord knew we would need each other."

"I guess He did," Gen said. "And you're right. I could use someone to talk to."

Betty smiled. "Want another cup of coffee first?"

"Sure," Gen said. And when Betty returned, two steaming mugs of coffee in her hands, Gen told her the story of her misguided marriage to Alton Gallier.

The part about Ellen, she decided to keep to herself, at least for now. Some secrets were harder to tell.

seven

Ernest shook off the cold and parked the roadster across the street from the corner grocery. In the ten days since he'd left Latanier, he'd been waiting for an "accidental" meeting with Genevieve Lamont. So far, the lovely lady hadn't made a single appearance at Mulotte's, and he had no other idea where to find her.

Leaning back in the seat, Ernest adjusted his cap and set to waiting. After a while, he blew on his hands, then stuffed his fists into the pockets of his winter coat.

If only the weather hadn't turned chilly. But that was spring in Louisiana. One day the skies were blue and the weather warm, and the next gray and cold. At least he'd timed his trip home to coincide with good weather.

Home. Ernest smiled. He'd had a good time in spite of himself back at the old place. With Mama and Papa and all the family in close quarters, he'd never expected to come back to his solitary room in New Iberia and miss the fun.

Why, even enduring the hour-long, white-knuckle Sunday afternoon ride with Papa at the wheel of the roadster seemed pleasant when remembered this afternoon.

He shivered. "Must be the cold turning me sentimental."

A flash of pink caught his attention, and he swiped at the foggy glass to clear the view. Sure enough, a young woman about Genevieve Lamont's size strolled past, dangling a handbag from her wrist. He would recognize that handbag anywhere. Why, if that wasn't the very purse Miss Lamont left on the floor of his roadster, he would eat his hat.

Ernest strained to see the bag's owner. Bundled in a coat

with a flowered scarf covering her hair and part of her face, he couldn't be sure it was Miss Lamont.

Still, he felt certain that was her purse.

For a moment he debated climbing out into the cold. As the woman neared the corner, he realized he'd either have to chase her down or lose sight of her. Compromising, he threw the car into gear and blended into traffic, rounding the corner just behind her. Easing the roadster to the curb, he leaned over to open the door.

"Miss Lamont?"

The woman jumped back, clutched her handbag to her chest, and whirled around to face him. It wasn't Miss Lamont.

"Sorry, ma'am," he said as he slammed the door and peeled away from the curb.

The ride back to his place took only a few minutes, but it seemed much longer. All the while he negotiated turns and steered around holes in the road, his mind was racing. What if he never saw Genevieve Lamont again? What if he said or did something that made her not want to see him again?

"That's ridiculous," he said as he climbed out of the roadster. The other issue, the issue of whether he might have offended her in some way, still concerned him. He sidestepped a puddle on the path to his door and shook his head. "You're just going to have to ask her yourself."

"Ask who?"

Ernest glanced over his shoulder to see his roommate, Phil Barker, coming up the walk behind him. "Just talking to myself," he said as he threw open the door and stepped inside.

Phil brushed past him to drop his coat and hat on the cot that served as his bed. His smile told Ernest he was about to comment.

"Got any coffee made?" Ernest asked quickly, hoping to head off a conversation he didn't intend to have.

"There's a little left in the pot from this morning, but I can't guarantee how it'll taste now."

"Doesn't matter as long as it's warm," Ernest said. "I hate

cold weather. It's April, for pity's sake."

"I've got a feeling the cold wouldn't bother you so much if you weren't pining away for a certain girl." Phil shook off his shoes and settled atop the blanket-covered mattress. "Why don't you tell old Phil all about her?"

Ernest poured the last of the thick black coffee into the first mug he could find, then took a healthy swig. True to his friend's warning, the coffee was more warm than tasty.

"Not much to tell, actually," he said. "And I'm not exactly pining away for her."

Phil rolled over onto his stomach and rested his chin in his hands. "All right then. What would you call it? You take the same drive at the same time every day; then you come back here to mope until bedtime. What gives?"

Nodding, Ernest set the mug beside the coffeepot. "I wish I knew. I mean, all I did was give her a ride to Latanier. We barely spoke, and what little she said indicated she had little interest in striking up a friendship with me."

"Aha!" Phil jumped to his feet and clapped Ernest on the shoulder. "That's it."

"That's what?"

Phil smiled. "It's like this. What do you usually do when a girl shows interest in you?"

Ernest settled at the table and removed his pocket change. "Is this a trick question?" He dropped three nickels and four pennies into the peanut butter jar labeled Rent that sat on the table.

"No. See, she's not interested in you, therefore you are very interested in her. All you have to do is spend more time with her, be properly charming until she falls for you, and voilà, you're cured, and she's out of your system." Phil clapped his hands, then reached for the one remaining mug on the shelf. "What is it like to live with someone so incredibly brilliant?"

"I wouldn't know." Ernest tossed his cap onto the table and shed his coat, then rose to trudge toward his bed. "I've spent the better part of a week trying to track her down, and she is nowhere to be found. So if you're so smart, you'd come up with a way to find her. After all, I can't get her out of my system if I don't know where she is."

Phil snapped his fingers. "Say, I think I have an idea."

Ernest stopped and whirled around to frown at his roommate. "Not another idea, please."

"No, this is a good one, I promise." He paused. "New Iberia is a big city. It stands to reason she'd be hard to find here. But back in Latanier, now that is someplace you'd know exactly where she would be, right?"

"Right," Ernest said slowly. "You know, Phil, I think I just might be about to figure out what it's like to live with someone incredibly brilliant."

"Well, of course. So, what are you going to do?"

"Do?" Ernest shrugged. "I'm busier than a one-legged man in a football-kicking contest down at the sawmill, and my boss said I can come in on my days off to work on a couple of projects I've been thinking of starting."

"What sort of projects?"

Ernest sank onto the sagging springs of his bed and tried to ignore their protest. "The boss said I could have the leftover lumber to make a few things with."

"You know, my friend, you are on the wrong end of the lumber business. I've never seen a man with such a talent for making things from wood." Phil pointed to the small chest sitting on the dresser they shared. "I can't believe you made that from discards you found in the trash bin."

The little oak box had been Ernest's "spare-time" project, a little something to fill his empty hours. He had to admit as he studied it that it had turned out quite nice.

"Now, back to this girl. I don't believe you told me her name."

Ernest returned his attention to Phil. "No, I don't believe I did."

"And you don't intend to, do you?" Phil waved away the question. "Forget I asked. I'll find out soon enough. Anyway, back to my original question of what you plan to do about her."

Good question. Too bad he had no answer.

Stretching, Ernest slipped off his shoes and let each drop with a *thud*. Finally he cast a glance over at Phil. Unfortunately, when his roommate bit into a topic, he tended to chew it until there was nothing left. He decided to give Phil an answer in hopes of ending the subject.

"You know, Phil, except for my trip home next weekend for my sister's birthday, I don't have any time off from work until the Fourth of July. Odds are, I won't remember her name next time I see her."

"Think so?"

Ernest knew he wouldn't forget her name or anything else about Genevieve Lamont, but there was no way he would admit it.

ঌ

Friday, May 5

Gen folded a napkin from the soda fountain around all but seven dollars of her monthly salary and stuffed it into an envelope along with a note for Big Mama. Tomorrow morning, she would mail the money and the letter on the way to work. *If only I'd remembered my extra stamps. I could buy more at the post office, but with the sparse funds I have for the month, it would be foolish to spend the extra money just to have the letter mailed today.*

Funny, three hundred dollars had seemed like a fortune when the check arrived. Now that April had slid past and May had arrived, the money had already begun to dwindle.

Taxes and Mother's medicines had taken a toll on the balance, leaving Gen to worry that at this rate there would be nothing left by the time Ellen started school. Of course, Big Mama reminded her that worrying didn't do a bit of good. She always backed the statement up with a favorite Bible verse; then she sweetened the discussion with a slice of pie.

Gen smiled. Big Mama was a blessing, all right, and without

her she'd be in quite a pickle. How a mama could work and take care of a baby was beyond her, although she knew of at least one girl at the five-and-dime who did. She'd taken to mentioning Dorothy in her prayers every night, and last payday she'd managed to slip a fifty-cent piece into Dorothy's pay envelope when she wasn't looking.

Fifty cents wasn't much, but given the amount of Gen's disposable income, it was practically the widow's mite. It had been fun to watch the girl open her paycheck and find the extra coins. She'd even played dumb when Dorothy asked about the true owner of the money.

What a blessing to be able to bless. The thought certainly brightened the dark times.

Today, however, nothing seemed to pierce the gloom. In the bottom of her purse was a letter from her landlord indicating the rent would go up substantially at the first of August. Where the extra funds would come from, she had no idea. Big Mama made the money Gen sent her stretch as far as she could. Rather than cut back there, Gen would just have to learn to live on less.

She cast a glance over at Dorothy, who had just finished placing a cherry atop a youngster's root beer float. *Lord, please allow someone else to bless her. It looks like my days of helping are over.*

A customer set a basket of items on the counter, distracting Gen. After she finished the transaction, she looked over to see Dorothy waving in her direction. Gen closed the cash register and headed toward the soda fountain.

Dorothy smiled. "I wanted to let you know I won't be coming back after today."

"Oh?"

The girl giggled and leaned toward Gen. "I'm getting married," she said softly. "Can you believe it?"

"Congratulations." Gen tried not to let her shock at the news color her excitement. "But I didn't know you were seeing anyone."

Dorothy shrugged. "It's the strangest thing. After Bobby's daddy died, I didn't think I would ever find happiness with another man. Then when I wasn't looking, the Lord surprised me with Ben." She paused. "Looks like Bobby and I finally have our family complete. Oh, Genevieve, I'm so happy."

"Well, that's wonderful, Dorothy."

She nodded. "I wanted to let you know first because without you, Ben and I would never have met."

"I don't understand."

"The extra money in my pay envelope—it took me awhile, but eventually I figured out it was from you." She smiled. "I thought it was quite a coincidence that you were always the last one to leave on payday."

"I suppose I'm not very good at that cloak-and-dagger stuff."

Dorothy touched Gen's arm. "You don't know how much I appreciated your donations. It made all the difference, and that's why I am telling you."

"I'm glad I could help, but I don't see how I had anything to do with your engagement."

Her friend's eyes sparkled. "Well, it's the funniest thing. After the first few weeks of getting that extra money in my pay envelope, I began to pray about what to buy with it. One day it hit me. Donate it. Well, that Sunday a man who supports missionary work in South America came to speak at church, and he told us all about this orphanage in Ecuador and the work the missionaries did there. I thought about little Bobby and how even though he didn't have a daddy, he did have a mama and how that was more than those little orphans had."

Gen nodded. This she knew firsthand to be true.

"When Ben wrote a note thanking me for my donation, I sent him a letter back, and that was how it all started. He came back to speak to us at church two weeks ago, and wouldn't you know it, he proposed to me right there in church last Sunday morning." She paused to shake her head. "Right there from the pulpit. Can you believe it? Oh, Genevieve, the first thing I did when I got home that night was to pray for you."

"For me?" Gen shook her head. "Why?"

"Because I feel like it's time for you to be the one who is blessed. It's your turn for happiness. I just know it."

Several responses begged to be spoken, but instead Gen chose to thank Dorothy and skitter back to the cash register. As she set back to work, she couldn't help hoping that maybe Dorothy's prayer for her might be heard and the wish granted.

By the time Gen stepped out of the five-and-dime into the brisk evening air, her black mood had lifted a bit. She thought about Dorothy and tried to imagine what it might feel like to be loved by a godly man. For all his positive traits—and Alton Gallier did have a few—no one would ever have mistaken him for a godly man.

This fault had seemed a minor one, something that would change once the marriage took place. To be sure, Alton attended church with her a time or two, and once she even caught him opening the pages of her Bible. Only later did she realize a man could sit in a church on Sunday morning and still find it permissible to hit his wife on Monday.

Gen suppressed a shudder and said a quick prayer that her husband had somehow gotten right with God before his untimely death. As much as she hated how he treated her, no one—not even Alton Gallier—should spend an eternity away from the Lord.

By morning, her mood had lifted altogether. Taking care not to wake Betty, who had the day off, Gen dressed quietly and tucked the letter to Big Mama into her handbag. At the corner, she slid the letter into the mailbox and let the lid shut with a resounding *clank*. As much as she hated being away from home and family, the one day each month when she sent money back to them made the other days worthwhile. Someday soon she would figure out a way to be with her daughter on more than just weekends. She'd petitioned the Lord on that subject too many times for Him to ignore her. In the meantime, she did her part in keeping the bills paid and food on the table.

If only she could sit at that table every night with the three women she loved more than any other in the world: Mother, Big Mama, and Ellen.

"Someday," she whispered as she whirled around and slammed directly into Ernest Breaux.

eight

Oh, no.

Gen took three steps back and shook her head. "I'm terribly sorry. I. . ." Surprise caught up with her, and she ran out of words.

"It's my fault, actually," Ernest said. "I should have said something."

"Yes, well. . ." Again, the words stopped. Gen felt like a fool and, most likely, looked like one, too. She smoothed her hair away from her face and tried hard to remember whether she'd taken the time to apply her usual powder and lipstick.

Probably not.

"You're up early for a Saturday morning," Ernest said.

Ignoring her better judgment, Gen focused her attention on the man standing before her. He did look quite stylish, what with his hair combed just so and his cap tilted back on his head. Why, if she didn't know better, she would think he'd dressed to go courting. A glance behind him revealed his flashy motorcar sitting at the curb. Even with her poor distance vision, there was no mistaking it.

Alton had always bragged about getting a car just like that one, something that would grab attention. Alton.

Gen's heart sank. Alton Gallier had been a handsome rogue with a pretty smile and polite manners. Why, until she married him, she never guessed what lay beneath the surface. Oh, Mother and Big Mama warned her, to be sure, but she never listened. After all, Alton had been so sweet and nice.

Just like Ernest Breaux.

Ernest gave her an expectant look and then a smile. My, but he did have a nice smile.

"Daydreaming?"

"Oh, well, I. . ." Gen frowned. Surely the man thought she was an idiot. "I'm sorry; what did you say?"

"I said, you're up early," he repeated.

Gen managed a nod. "Yes, well, I suppose I am."

Her lower lip quivered, and she bit it so hard it felt like she drew blood. Just to be sure, she swiped her hand across her mouth. *Nothing. Good. Now to escape.*

Casting a glance around, she prayed for a distraction so she could slip away unnoticed. Except for a pair of lazy hound dogs sunning themselves in front of the barbershop and an elderly woman sweeping the sidewalk in front of the church, the streets of New Iberia were deserted.

She swung her attention back to Ernest. Was she mistaken, or did he look as uncomfortable as she felt?

"Mailing letters back home?"

"Yes, actually." Gen squared her shoulders and thrust her hand in his direction. "Well, it was nice running into you." She groaned at the accidental reference to their collision. "I mean, it was nice seeing you."

Before she could make a fool of herself any further, Gen slipped past Ernest. To her dismay, he fell in step beside her.

"In a hurry?"

"I'm heading to work," she said.

"Ah." He continued to keep pace with her, slowing his long stride to match hers. "So, do you work all day?"

Giving him a sideways glance, she nodded.

"Until what time?"

Gen stopped short at the corner across from the church, and Ernest followed suit. "You ask a lot of questions. Did you realize that?"

Ernest looked perplexed. "I do?"

Again she nodded.

"Should I apologize?"

He looked so contrite that she couldn't give him the sharp answer she intended. The truth was Ernest Breaux seemed like a genuinely nice man.

But then so did Alton Gallier.

"No," she said. "There's no need to apologize. Just stop, all right?"

She headed for the corner and turned to cross the street. The elderly woman had stopped her sweeping to watch, and Gen offered her a quick smile. She nodded and grasped her broom to return to work.

"Wait," Ernest called as Gen reached the other side. "I'd like to see you again."

"Why?"

The question was out before she realized she had said it aloud. Not only had she said it, she'd actually shouted it across the street. Color flooded her cheeks as heat filled her face.

One more reason not to take up again with a man. She was no good at it.

࣪ঌ

Why, indeed.

Ernest pondered the question for a full minute, all the while expecting Miss Lamont to scurry back to that place where she'd been hiding all week. To his surprise, she remained rooted to the spot, no doubt enjoying his discomfort.

"Well, now, Miss Genevieve, that is a good question. Why *would* I want to see you again?"

He scratched his head and pretended to consider it. Actually, the only trouble he had with answering was how much to say and what to say first, but he'd never tell her that. Before he could sort out his thoughts and give her a brilliant answer, she had the audacity to turn around and walk away.

"Never mind," she said with a wave of her hand. "I'm sure I will see you around. Good-bye, Mr. Breaux."

For a split second he thought of following her, of using his considerable charm to woo her into continuing their conversation. He certainly had no trouble making small talk with the ladies. Then his brain caught up with his pride, and he stopped. Better to approach this situation with care—and a little planning.

Why, he wouldn't hack at just any old oak tree in order to get lumber for a chair or cut down the closest pecan tree to find wood for a table. No, he would choose the best trees, take time to study them, and then treat them with care.

The same would go for Genevieve Lamont. Taking the time to approach her carefully would be his plan. He would study her and figure out just the right way to get to know her.

For, like a piece of fine furniture, she obviously had great value.

Ernest smiled at the comparison. The woman in question would probably not appreciate being compared to a nicely crafted table or chair. Still, he could think of no greater compliment.

Maybe Papa was right. Deep down he was probably made to be a furniture maker. Unfortunately, he had bills to pay, and as satisfying as it would be to chuck all his responsibilities and play with wood and chisel all day, he couldn't put gasoline in the roadster with an empty wallet.

These days, having a job at all was a blessing. How could he think of walking away to pursue a dream, especially one with so little chance of succeeding?

Ernest shook his head and captured his wits. If he didn't hurry, he would lose sight of the lovely Miss Genevieve. He thought of jumping in the roadster to catch up to her but decided to do the job on foot. Besides, he could hardly be discreet in something so snazzy.

He adjusted his cap and headed off. Up ahead he saw the object of his thoughts disappear into the five-and-dime. She said she was up early for work, so it was possible this was where she worked.

Or she could be doing a little shopping first.

Checking his watch, he realized the store had not yet opened. Unless she were employed there, it was highly unlikely Genevieve Lamont would be allowed inside.

"Work it is," Ernest said as he doubled back to climb inside the roadster. He paused to crank the engine then eased the car away from the curb. As he turned to drive past the five-and-dime, he tried to look casual while peering into the windows in hopes of seeing Genevieve.

No sight of her greeted him, but that did not matter. "At least I know how to find her."

Ernest smiled at the turn of events that led him to meet up with the lovely lady that morning. After working a double shift, he'd arrived home with the sunrise. Although the temptation to fall into bed was strong, he'd forced himself to change clothes and head for the mailbox with his little sister's birthday letter. With the slow speed of bayou mail, Amalie might miss receiving her letter if he put off mailing it until Monday.

"Thank you, Amalie," he said under his breath as he made the turn at the end of the block and headed back home. "Oh, and thank You, Lord." He paused to allow a mama dog and two puppies to cross the road. "And as long as You are thinking of me, God, would You do just one more thing? Would You grant me some patience where Miss Lamont is concerned? I'm thinking I just might need all I can muster to keep from bothering her until she sees what a great catch I am."

Catch? Ernest guided the roadster to the curb in front of his place then shut off the engine, suppressing a shudder. Since when had his interest in the pretty girl from Latanier moved from a possible date to something else?

All the more reason to keep in close contact with the Lord. After all, He wouldn't let Ernest make the mistake of falling in love with a woman he barely knew.

He wouldn't, would He?

nine

Wednesday, May 10

Ernest had used about all the patience he could stand. He paced the sidewalk in front of the five-and-dime, nearly wearing a rut in the concrete before he finally decided to save on shoe leather and go inside. A second before his hand touched the polished brass doorknob, he said a quick prayer that the Lord would smile on him as he tried his best to spend time with Miss Lamont.

Once inside, he cast about for the object of his pacing. Rather than find her, he saw an oversized man with a head full of greasy hair and a belly that rivaled Papa's prize sow. The fellow frowned before rising from his perch at the soda fountain to greet Ernest.

"Something I can help you with?" He pulled a toothpick out of his shirt pocket and began to work it between his front teeth. "I'm Lester Bonfils, the manager around here."

"No, thank you," Ernest said. "I'm just looking right now."

The man looked him up and down, then gave a snort before turning to climb back on his stool.

"I see you've met Lester."

Ernest whirled around to see a pretty, dark-haired woman who looked to be about his age standing beside a toothpaste display. "Yes, I did."

"He runs things around here, or at least we let him think he does." She smiled. "I'm Betty. Let me know if there's anything I can help you with."

Ernest looked past Betty to where a vision in pink caught his eye. There she stood, Genevieve Lamont, making change for the mayor's wife. As she finished the transaction and closed the cash drawer, her gaze collided with his.

"Something wrong, sir?"

He returned his attention to Betty, who stared at him with a perplexed look. "No, nothing," he said. "But I think I've found what I was looking for."

Rather than go directly up to Miss Lamont, Ernest took a roundabout path that led him through several aisles. By the time he reached the front of the store, he'd accumulated two packages of baking soda, a box of saltine crackers, and a pair of black shoelaces for his church shoes. As he dumped the items on the counter, he fitted a casual look onto his face and studied the ceiling.

"Ernest?"

He lowered his gaze to meet hers. "Genevieve Lamont. What in the world are you doing here?"

The pink of her cheeks and lips matched the color of her spring dress. "I work here."

She paused and seemed to be trying to collect herself. Or at least that's what Ernest hoped as he struggled to slow his racing pulse.

"Well, now, how about that?" he managed.

An awkward silence fell between them. Finally Genevieve reached for the package of shoelaces and began to punch in the price on the cash register. At the rate she was going, she would be finished in no time. Soon he'd have to hand her his money, take his things, and leave the five-and-dime. He'd have no excuse for standing there and staring or making small talk.

If he could manage small talk, that is.

He should do something. Say something. Anything to stop her before she placed his last item in the bag.

"Wait."

As soon as he said it, Ernest felt like a fool. Now what? The prettiest girl in New Iberia stood right in front of him holding a box of baking soda and, at the same time, capturing his heart.

"Yes? Did you forget something?"

"Actually, well, I. . ." He reached back to grab a tube of toothpaste off the shelf, ignoring the strange look Betty gave him. "I need toothpaste," he said with a shrug.

As quickly as he handed her the toothpaste, she rang it up and dropped it into the bag with the other items. "Anything else?"

What now? He darted his eyes to the left and then back to the right. A display of brightly colored papers and pens caught his attention. "Oh, and a birthday present for my sister."

"Do you know what she would like?"

"Hmmm," he said. "I really don't have any idea. Would you mind helping?" There, that ought to buy him some time. "Maybe just giving me an opinion of what a girl about to turn thirteen might like for her birthday," he added for good measure.

"I suppose." She gave him a tentative look, and his heart doubled its pace. "Tell me a little about your sister. What does she like to do? Does she have any favorite activities?"

"Let's see." Ernest scratched his head. "She loves to read." He paused to think, something made extremely difficult with Genevieve Lamont's dark eyes staring in his direction. "Oh, and she says she wants to be a writer someday, but I've always said she ought to go to California and act in the movies. She just can't get enough of them."

"Well, let's see. Unless you're planning to make a special day of it at the Evangeline Theater, I'm afraid the only thing on that list is books."

"Books." He nodded. "Yes, I think that would work just fine."

Genevieve set the bag of items aside and cleared the register, then indicated for him to follow her. Two aisles over, she stopped in front of a shelf filled with books of all sorts. He picked up one by Zane Grey that looked nifty but replaced it on the shelf when he saw Genevieve's frown.

"Maybe you ought to help me with this, what with you being a pretty girl and all." Ernest felt the heat climb into his neck. Of all the things to say. "What I mean is, you're a female and she is, too."

He dared a glance in her direction and saw her lips tilt into a smile for the briefest of seconds. For all his blundering, at least he hadn't offended her.

Yet.

"What about this one? Girls seem to love the Nancy Drew series." She moved past him, and he smelled the scent of roses. "This is the third in the series, and there are the first two. There are more titles, but we're a little slow getting them."

Ernest reached for the book and weighed it in his hand. "You recommend this for teenage girls? I mean, look at her." He pointed to the girl in the blue dress on the cover. "Looks like she's snooping around."

Genevieve stifled a giggle. "She's supposed to be snooping, Ernest. This is a mystery novel."

"Well, that explains it." He reached for the other two books with the blue-dressed girl on the cover. "Might as well get all three of them. She'll probably finish these before I know it and be asking for the next one. That Amalie reads as fast as anyone I know."

"Reading is a good way to keep a young girl out of trouble." Genevieve reached past him to fill the empty spot on the shelf with another copy. "I have to admit I like them, too. Only I have to check mine out from the library."

"If Latanier had a library, Amalie would take a pillow and blanket and live there." Ernest chuckled. "Since they don't, I guess I'll just have to keep coming in here and buying books for her."

Rather than speak, she looked away. Ernest ran out of words, and an awkward silence fell between them.

"Excuse me, Miss Lamont, but if you're finished helping this gentleman, I could use you back at your job at the cash register."

Ernest whirled around to see Lester Bonfils blocking the end of the aisle, the toothpick planted in the gap between his front teeth. "Actually, Miss Lamont was just about to help me with a Western novel." He turned back to face Genevieve and forced a serious look. "Do you have anything by Zane Grey?"

"Yes, actually, we do, Mr. Breaux. Mr. Grey's newest one is right here." Genevieve reached for the novel Ernest had just put back on the shelf and placed it atop the three Nancy Drew novels in his arms. "I wonder if you might also like his last book. Where is it? Oh, there it is." She grabbed another book off the shelf and added it to his stack, trying not to smile. "This one seems to sell well among our gentleman customers."

"I see." He pursed his lips to keep from laughing. "While I'm at it, is there anything else you'd recommend?"

"Well, I don't know, sir. You see, Mr. Bonfils is the manager, and I think he may need me to go back up to the register."

Ernest cast a glance over his shoulder to look at Lester. "I don't know if you realize this, but Miss Lamont here is very knowledgeable about books. If she can't spend a few more minutes helping me with my reading material, then I'm afraid I'll have to put these back on the shelf and return when she has more time."

His statement seemed to have no effect on the portly manager, so Ernest tried another strategy. "Or maybe you could help me. I've been looking for a nice book on flower arranging. I wonder if you have something like that. I do love a nice arrangement of flowers when I come home from a hard day."

Lester's face registered a blank look. "Flower arranging? I leave that to the ladies."

"Then until I can find a lady who's not too busy to advise me, I will just have to take my business elsewhere."

Before Ernest could make good on his threat, Lester Bonfils was gone. "See that you get yourself back to the register soon as you're done, Miss Lamont," he said as he disappeared around a display of Alka-Seltzer.

"Yes, sir," Genevieve called. "Right away, Mr. Bonfils."

He gave Genevieve a penitent look. "Did I get you in trouble?"

"Trouble?" She shrugged. "Now, about that book on flower arranging."

"Oh. That. See, actually I'm not much for arranging flowers.

Actually, I'm not much for flowers at all." He shook his head. "That's not true. I mean, I like flowers, but I don't really find much need to. . ." Ernest gave up. "I'm rambling, aren't I?"

Big brown eyes continued to peer up at him, her expression giving away nothing of her thoughts. "Yes, actually, you are."

He looked away, out of words. To his surprise, he felt Genevieve touch his arm.

"I should get back to work."

"I could find more to buy." Ernest juggled his books and tucked them into a stack under his arm. He gestured toward the Alka-Seltzer display. "What about those? After all this reading I just might need something for indigestion."

Genevieve's grin broadened. "You're funny."

"Miss Lamont? Could you come here?"

Lester Bonfils stood beside the soda fountain, one hand on his hip and a frown on his face. Ernest watched as Genevieve scurried over and endured a crisp instruction to man the counter rather than return to the cash register. As a final insult, Lester caught Ernest's gaze, seemingly daring him to complain.

A few choice words came to mind, but Ernest swallowed them along with his pride. A job was a precious thing, and he wouldn't dare do or say anything to cause Genevieve to lose hers. The Bonfils fellow must have known this because he walked away from the soda fountain chuckling.

Ernest checked the clock above the fountain. It read a quarter to one. He was set to work the night shift at the sawmill, so he had nowhere to go until ten. Of course, he'd need to find time to get some sleep before then, but he had all afternoon for that.

With a grin, he headed for the cash register to pay for his purchases. The young lady behind the counter, what was her name? She'd introduced herself when he first walked into the five-and-dime, but he'd paid little attention.

Barbara? No, maybe it was Brenda. As he neared the register, he saw that her name tag read Betty.

Yes, that was it. Betty.

Out of the corner of his eye, Ernest thought he saw Genevieve watching him; but when he turned to check, she'd looked away.

"My, but you must be quite a reader."

Setting the books on the counter, Ernest reached for his wallet. "I suppose it would seem that way, Betty, but I'm here buying birthday gifts." He cast a glance over his shoulder to find Genevieve casually cleaning a soda glass.

"Birthday gifts, huh?" Betty chuckled. "My guess is you had more on your mind than birthdays when you walked in here."

Ernest felt the heat rise in his neck. Without comment, he peeled off the cash and handed it to Betty. He'd almost made it out the door when he had a thought.

He sure was thirsty.

Adjusting his cap, Ernest sized up his options. He could head for home and slake his thirst with a cold drink of water, or he could walk down the street to Mulotte's Grocery and buy a bottle of cola. He could even take a table at the new hamburger joint around the corner where there was a large choice of beverages.

Or he could belly up to the soda fountain and have something right now.

It didn't take him long to decide which option appealed the most. Within seconds, he'd claimed the nearest stool to Genevieve Lamont and ordered a soda water with vanilla and a cherry.

"I can't visit with you any more, you know." She looked around the perimeter of the store then returned her gaze to Ernest. "I can't afford to lose this job, and Mr. Bonfils is looking for any excuse to fire me."

"Well, first off, the man must be out of his mind to want to banish such a lovely lady from the premises. And second. . ." He paused to take a long draw of soda water. "I'm a working man myself, and I know how precious a paycheck can be. You have my word that I won't interfere with your making a living."

Relief flooded her face. "Thank you."

"Don't mention it." Ernest faked an impatient look as he finished the last sip of water in the glass. "Now, where's my refill?"

"You're teasing me, aren't you?"

"Miss Lamont, I am a thirsty man with a book to read." He selected the Zane Grey novel and cracked it open to the first chapter. "So fetch my soda. I've got outlaws to catch."

"Yes, sir," she said as she stifled a giggle.

Genevieve seemed amused when he ordered his third drink and concerned when he asked for a fourth. By the fifth soda water, his stomach had begun to complain and so had Lester Bonfils. Trouble with Mr. Bonfils's complaints was that Ernest was a paying customer and there wasn't a thing that could be done about it.

By the time six o'clock rolled around, Ernest had finished his sixth soda water and nearly completed the Zane Grey novel. He'd also decided that Genevieve Lamont worked far too hard and was due an evening off.

Perhaps an evening with him.

They could have supper at the little burger joint then head to the Evangeline Theater to see what was playing. If he had her home by nine thirty, he could still make it to work on time.

True, he'd work tonight without sleep, but the time spent with Genevieve Lamont would be worth it.

He almost missed his chance to tell her that. As he gathered his books, she slipped out the front door. Ernest caught up with her on the sidewalk.

"Where are you going?" he called, adjusting his stack of books to keep from decorating the sidewalk with them.

At first she seemed not to hear, but a moment later she stopped and turned around to face him. The good humor she had displayed in the five-and-dime was gone.

ten

"Are you following me?"

"What?" Ernest stopped short when Genevieve repeated the question. "Following? No, I was. . ." He shook his head. "I can't tell a lie. Yes, I was following you. But I had a good reason."

Genevieve's expression told him she had doubts. She said nothing, however.

"Yes, see, I just wanted to ask you. . ." His tongue stuck on the roof of his mouth, and his voice disappeared. A moment later, he cleared his throat and tried again. "What do you say to a movie tonight?"

There, he'd said it. Before he could feel relieved that he'd managed the invitation, terror took over. She hadn't answered.

Instead, she stood stock-still, looking like she'd just swallowed a bug. Unless he missed his guess, she'd just heard the worst question of her life.

Ernest was about to apologize for the intrusion and head for home to lick his wounds when the most amazing thing happened. She smiled.

Then she said, "Not tonight."

His hopes plummeted. "Oh," was all he could manage.

She looked up at him and blinked hard. Was that the beginnings of a smile he saw?

"What about tomorrow night?"

Considering the ache in his gut, tomorrow was probably the better choice. Still, he felt more than a little disappointment at the wait. He parted company with her after agreeing to meet on the steps of the five-and-dime at half past six.

But not before he tried and failed to convince Gen to let him walk her home.

Later, as he lay facedown on his bed, he asked his roommate,

Phil, if he thought it strange that a woman wouldn't reveal where she lived to a gentleman.

"Depends," Phil said. "She could be hiding something, but as a rule I'd have to say she's probably just the cautious type."

Ernest rolled over on his back, then groaned when his stomach complained. "Maybe," he said, "but her people have known my people for a hundred years. More, actually. I know where she lives in Latanier, and what I don't know about her, I could find out from my mother or one of my sisters. Why would it matter that I know where she lives in New Iberia?"

Phil gave Ernest a look. "Why indeed," he said slowly.

Ernest rolled up on his elbows then forced himself into a sitting position. Thankfully his stomach seemed to like sitting better than lying down. "What does that mean?"

"Nothing."

"Go on and say it."

"All right." Phil shrugged. "It's just that the way you've been carrying on lately, well, a body'd think you were about to fall hard for that girl. And you know the next step after a man falls. He starts hearing wedding bells."

Ernest laughed again. "Oh, that's a good one, my friend. Me married?"

"Don't sound so confident. Better men than you have taken that road. I hear some of them actually enjoy married life. Just a rumor, of course."

"Never, Phil," Ernest said. "You forget that I'm the oldest of a dozen children. Mama and Papa gave up all they had to raise young'uns. I don't plan to make that kind of sacrifice— leastwise not while I'm young enough to appreciate the finer things in life. I'm a woodworker, Phil, and someday I intend to have a nice furniture shop, maybe a little place where a man can buy a table and chairs or a bench that lasts. No, sir, I intend to make baby cribs—not families."

Phil said nothing.

"You don't believe me, do you?"

"It doesn't matter whether I believe you or not. You're falling for that girl from the five-and-dime, and you seem to be the only one who hasn't figured that out."

"Am not."

But was he? His aching gut would protest the statement. Why else would a sane, rational man down six soda waters in one afternoon when he ought to be home catching up on his sleep? It sure wasn't because the book was so good, although he had to admit Mr. Grey could tell a whopper of a tale.

No, he sat on that hard stool drinking cherry vanilla soda waters one after the other because he couldn't bring himself to leave the five-and-dime. Rather than be away from Genevieve Lamont, he'd chosen to sit in her presence and make a fool of himself.

Was that love?

He'd never know because he refused to fall in love.

True, Genevieve was a nice girl; and true again, he did enjoy her company. And tomorrow night, well, it really wasn't a date. Actually it was more like two neighbors from Latanier meeting to pass a good time.

Well, whatever it was, Ernest certainly didn't know Genevieve well enough to figure out how to classify her. So maybe tomorrow night would be just a getting-to-know-you visit.

Yes, that was it.

For the first time since he'd ordered the afternoon's sodas, he felt better. Not that his gut had stopped complaining, for it hadn't, but he actually had the beginnings of a plan.

Ernest would spend some time with Genevieve, maybe have a laugh or two, then that would be the end of it. Surely whatever interest he felt would fade once he had a clearer picture of the mysterious Miss Lamont.

❧

"Genevieve, I don't remember when I've seen you so nervous, hon." Betty stepped away from the window to touch Gen's sleeve. "Why, you look like you're about to jump out of your skin."

Gen loosened her scarf and set her handbag beside the door.

"I guess I am a little out of sorts."

Betty gestured toward the window. "Coffee on the terrace?"

"Sure," Gen said. "But let me change first."

She slipped out of her working clothes and into a simple housedress that Big Mama had fashioned out of rose-printed potato sacks. As she closed the wardrobe, she caught sight of herself in the mirror. Or rather, she saw a stranger staring back.

Gen touched the rough cotton fabric then allowed her hands to fall at her sides, resting against hips a bit more padded since Ellen's birth. Loose tendrils of dark hair fell at her temples, resisting capture into the bun at the back of her neck.

Gen leaned in to look into that woman's eyes. Despite her age, the person in the mirror looked old. Not old in the sense that many years had passed, but old in that she had lived many years in a short time.

Where had the silly girl with the head full of dreams gone?

The woman-child who believed anything was possible had realized the downside of that truth. When anything became possible, anything could happen. And sometimes, what happened wasn't what you expected.

"Gen, honey. You all right?"

"I'm fine." Gen smoothed the loose curls back into her bun and reached for a pair of bobby pins to keep them in place. "I'll be there in a sec."

"Don't take too long. The coffee's getting cold."

A trip down the hall to the only bathroom in the building kept Gen from sipping coffee that was steaming hot, but the temperature of the dark brew didn't matter. It was the warmth of friendship that counted right then.

And she really needed a friend. In short order, she finished her coffee and the story about the afternoon's visit with Ernest Breaux. Finally she admitted she'd agreed to a movie date with him.

A cool breeze blew across Gen as she curled her legs beneath her and waited for Betty's response. What her roommate would make of the situation was anyone's guess, but Gen had the highest respect for her opinion.

Betty chuckled. "I wondered if he would stay all afternoon. I mean, it couldn't have been much after twelve thirty when the man walked into the store, and there he still sat with a half-empty soda and that book when I went home at three."

"Well, he tried to follow me home at six, so you do the math."

"That's a long time to sit in one place." Betty sipped at the remains of her coffee. "I don't have to think too hard to come up with a reason why a man would do that. What about you?"

Gen avoided her friend's direct gaze. "I suppose it's possible the book was exceptionally good and he liked the soda waters."

"I suppose." Betty rose and climbed inside to return with the coffeepot. She filled their mugs then set the pot beside her. "Is he a nice man? Does he come from good people?"

Gen thought of his behavior at the bus station and his concern over her riding the bus. "Yes, he appears to be very nice. A real gentleman, actually, from a good family."

"He's a bit older than you, isn't he?"

"Let me think." She tried to guess his age compared to his siblings. "A few years, seven or eight at the most, I would suppose, but I know he's not yet thirty. Now *that* would be old."

Betty made a face. "It won't seem so old when you're as close to it as I am." She paused and seemed to be deep in thought. "You know, hon, it seems to me that you're afraid of something."

"Afraid?"

Nodding, Betty stared past Gen. "You have a movie date with a nice man, a gentleman, who isn't too old or too young and whose family you know and like, right?"

She blew on the steaming coffee then took a sip. "Right."

"So what's wrong with that?" Betty rested her elbows on her knees. "I mean, sure, you've been through it, what with marrying that fellow, then having your heart broken and all, but are you going to spend the rest of your life being afraid to go out and try again?"

Gen considered the question for half a second before she dismissed it. Rising, she scooped up her mug and headed inside to wash it in the tiny sink.

"Come on, hon, don't run off." Betty followed her inside and set her coffee cup beside Gen's in the sink. She touched Gen's sleeve and shook her head. "The Lord doesn't make us to fear anyone or anything but Him."

"I know that." But did she? Hadn't she spent a good part of the last year in fear?

Betty nudged her with her elbow. "So take what you know and put it into practice."

"That's easy for you to say." Gen set the mugs to dry on the drain board then leaned against the counter. "You really don't think going out on a date is awful." She paused. "I mean, considering."

Her roommate shrugged. "Considering what?"

"My secrets, Betty. I've got more than my share, wouldn't you say?"

"How much does this fellow know about your past?"

Gen paused to think. "About as much as the rest of Latanier knows, I suppose. I was raised there then left home after I finished school. I doubt Mother bragged about my running off with Alton, and I know for a fact that my father never said a word about it."

"So it's likely your date doesn't know he's taking a widow to the movies."

"That's right." Gen wrapped her arms around her middle. "I'm confused, Betty. He's nice, and I think I could really enjoy spending time with him. On the other hand, I've felt this way before."

"With Alton?"

Gen nodded. "And it's not just me that I have to be worried about. The Lord gave me. . ." She bit down on the last of her statement and looked away. As much as she longed to confide in Betty, to tell her about the precious baby girl she missed every moment she was away from her, Gen couldn't say a word. Not yet. Some secrets were too precious.

"That's what you're afraid of, isn't it? That this man will turn out the same way, and you'll be back in a place where God never meant you to be."

How simple the trouble sounded when Betty summed it up. And how terribly complicated it was.

"Yes."

Betty seemed to ponder the point a moment. "Were you thinking of marrying this one, too?"

"No," Gen said. "Of course not."

Betty gave Gen a satisfied smile. "In that case, I say go out and have a good time. Allow yourself that much, hon. You deserve a little fun, what with the way you work so hard." She paused. "But would you do one thing for me first?"

"Of course," Gen said. "What's that?"

"Pray about the date, and ask the Lord to guide you in the matter. If He doesn't want this, you shouldn't either. Ask Him and see what He says."

That night as Gen lay awake, she took Betty's advice. Rather than receive an answer from the Lord on her predicament, she was met with silence.

Finally, she gave up and closed her eyes. As she drifted somewhere between sleep and dreams, she felt a stirring of hope. If silence was all that greeted her, maybe the Lord was trying to tell her she'd made the wrong choice.

"Father," she whispered into her pillow, "between You and me, I don't know if I will ever be finished with that old life, even if You did take Alton home. I'm not going to expect an answer tonight, but if You want me to get on with my life like Betty said I should, would You mind sending me a message real plainlike?"

eleven

Thursday, May 11

Six o'clock straight up. Fifteen minutes to go, and her nerves were already jittery. The five-and-dime's doors swung open. Gen fought the urge to run inside and hide, to somehow make herself invisible until time passed and Ernest Breaux gave up and went home.

She should never have borrowed this dress from Betty. Green was absolutely not a good color for her. Why, as she looked at her reflection in the window of the five-and-dime, there was no mistaking the fact that she looked like a stick of celery.

And why in the world had she chosen to bring that old white sweater? She removed the sweater and tied it around her shoulders, then smoothed her hair back into place.

My, but she needed a trim. Or maybe she shouldn't have worn her hair down. Just wait until she saw Betty tonight. Listening to her about the dress and her hair had been the wrong thing to do.

She took a deep breath and let it out slowly. Searching for something to calm herself, Gen began to repeat the prayer she'd begun last night. "And they that know thy name will put their trust in thee: for thou, Lord, hast not forsaken them that seek thee," she whispered, claiming the promise from Psalm 9 as her own.

Funny how she'd held on to that verse since she was a little girl only to forget all about it when Alton Gallier came into her life. But then she'd forgotten about a lot of things she'd once held onto when Alton came along.

"It is finished."

The words were as clear as if someone had whispered them in her ear. Gen looked to the right and the left. Other than the usual busyness of the New Iberia evening, no one stood near enough to speak.

"It is finished."

She jumped. While she regularly carried on lengthy conversations with the heavenly Father, not once had she had an actual reply—at least not one she could practically hear. She slipped around the side of the building and leaned against the brick wall.

"Lord," she whispered, "is that You?"

"Let it be finished."

"It, Lord?"

"The past. It is finished."

Gen shook her head then began to giggle. Well, there it was. Her answer. The God of all the universe had taken the time to speak directly to her. She continued to giggle even as the tears flowed.

All at once her body felt light, and it seemed as though years of living fell away. She felt like a child, a little girl finally allowed to go out and play after a long, cold winter indoors.

Wiping her eyes with the corner of her handkerchief, Gen gathered her wits and took a deep breath. Letting it out slowly, she headed toward the front of the five-and-dime.

"I didn't think you were coming."

Ernest Breaux smiled down at her from the top step. "I'm terribly sorry," she said as she carefully tucked her handkerchief into her skirt pocket.

He met her on the sidewalk and let out a low whistle. "You look beautiful. I don't believe I've ever seen such a pretty shade of green on a lady."

Gen blushed, a strange feeling for a widowed mother. "Thank you," she said. "You look nice, too."

As soon as she said the words, she felt the heat flame hotter in her cheeks. He did look nice—awfully nice, actually—and he smelled nice, too.

But to tell him so? And on a first date? What an idiot he must think her to be.

⋙

She must think I'm an idiot.

Ernest stifled a groan at the stupid comment he'd made. Of course she looked nice. Actually, she looked more than nice. Couldn't he have commented on something besides her looks? True, she was the prettiest girl in New Iberia, but surely she already knew that.

And while her looks first caught his attention, her sweet spirit, contagious laughter, and genuine personality were what kept him interested.

He looked down at her and his breath caught. Was that a tear he saw in the corner of her eye?

"Are you all right?"

She considered the question a moment longer than he liked, but when she answered, she smiled first. "Yes, I'm fine," she said. "Why?"

Now what to say? That she looked like she'd been crying? Oh, no. Ernest had too many sisters not to know better than that.

"No reason," he said as he offered her his hand. "Shall we?"

At first he thought she might say no, or worse, she might say nothing at all and just hightail it out of there. Instead, she looked at his hand like it had grown a second thumb.

Then she smiled.

It wasn't a real smile, actually. Not one of those broad grins that a body can't help but make. No, this was more like something she did because she knew she was supposed to.

Ernest expelled a long breath and looked away. "You sure you want to be here tonight? With me, I mean."

He swung his gaze back to collide with Genevieve's. This time the smile seemed genuine.

"I'm afraid you caught me," she said as she studied her hands.

Ernest's heart sank. Looked like the evening would be over before it got started. "Oh," he managed. "How's that?"

Once again, she met his stare. "I'm nervous, Ernest. I haven't gone out with a boy. . ." Her voice faltered and she cleared her throat. "I mean, a man," she continued, "in so long I'm not sure I remember how."

"You?" He could tell his question startled her. "I mean, a girl as pretty and smart as you must have a whole lot of fellows moonstruck. Why, I'd be willing to bet you are putting me on."

"I'm serious, Ernest. I'm afraid I might not be very good company for you this evening." She shook her head. "I just don't know what I'm doing here."

He took two steps back and stuffed his fists into his pockets. "Well, now, that's a mite disappointing. But I think I can help you with that."

She gave him a confused look. "I don't understand."

"Well, Miss Lamont, it's like this." He gestured to the step where she stood. "You're at the five-and-dime, and I'm over here on the sidewalk." When she nodded, he continued, pointing north. "Over yonder is the movie theater. You ever been to one of those? Big building with lots of pretty lights."

"Yes, I'm familiar with them." Her lips turned up in a slight grin. "I've actually been a time or two."

"Good, then I don't have to explain how to sit in the seat and watch the movie, and you won't get upset when the lights go out." Ernest rocked back on his heels. "Now, Miss Lamont, have you ever had candy? It's that sweet stuff they sell behind the counter in those movie theaters you've been to."

The grin inched up and almost became a smile. "Yes, I've had candy, Mr. Breaux, although I'm partial to watching movies without the interruption of having to chew."

"Excellent." He took a step forward and put on a perplexed look. "There's just one more thing. How proud were you of that streak you had going?"

"Streak?"

Ernest nodded. "All that time without a date. Will it bother you terribly to end that streak? Because I believe you're about to."

Her smile became a giggle and then a full-sized laugh. "You

know," she said as she met Ernest on the sidewalk, "I don't believe it will bother me at all."

"Then I will repeat my original question." Ernest offered Genevieve his hand. "Shall we?"

This time she accepted his offer, and when Genevieve touched him, he felt like he could conquer the world.

Strolling through New Iberia making small talk about the weather and the folks back in Latanier felt even better. By the time he'd bought two tickets for *Me and My Pal*, the new Laurel and Hardy film, and settled four rows back from the screen, the feeling had grown to the point where he couldn't stop smiling if he tried.

Good thing they'd chosen a comedy.

Not that he watched a bit of the movie. No, he was too busy sneaking glances at Genevieve, who seemed to be enjoying herself despite sitting so close to the screen that she had to lean back and look up.

Once or twice he considered snaking his arm around the back of Genevieve's seat, but he decided against it. With their friendship so new and tender, Ernest dared not do anything so familiar.

No, this lady was skittish as a newborn colt. She probably had good reason, although Ernest doubted it had been as long as Genevieve led him to believe since she'd had a date.

That was impossible to believe. There weren't that many stupid men in Iberia Parish; surely one of the smart ones had seen what Ernest saw when he looked at Genevieve.

He glanced back at the screen in time to see Mr. Hardy take a fall, then joined Genevieve in laughter. "Does it bother you to sit so close?" he whispered when the laughter died.

She cast a worried glance in his direction. "No," she said as she reached for her purse, "but we can move if you'd like."

"No, I'm fine." He offered a weak smile to go along with the wishful thinking. His head was beginning to throb due to the closeness of the screen. Not that he would ever let Genevieve know.

Too soon the movie ended, and Ernest found himself ushering his date through the lobby toward the glass doors and the street beyond. Without warning, Genevieve stopped and turned around.

"What's wrong?" he asked as he tagged a half step behind her.

She came to a halt in front of the candy counter. "One of those, please," he heard her say.

Before Ernest could react, Genevieve had requested two candy bars and handed over her dime. Whirling around to face him, she offered him a big smile and a Milky Way bar. He sputtered a word of thanks.

What an interesting woman.

"Shall we?" she asked.

Ernest tucked the candy into his shirt pocket. "Lead the way, m'lady," he said as he offered a mock bow.

They settled across the street from the theater on a park bench. While the last of the moviegoers filed out beneath the lighted marquee, Ernest enjoyed the best candy bar he'd had in years.

And he didn't even like candy.

But somehow sitting next to Genevieve while she obviously enjoyed hers made all the difference. Ernest heaved a long sigh and looked past the theater to the stars, nearly hidden by the brilliance of a thousand lights.

"It's a beautiful night," Genevieve said.

Ernest nodded, turning his attention from the stars to the lovely lady at his side. "Yes," he said softly, "beautiful indeed."

If she caught the compliment, she gave no indication. Rather, she continued to nibble on her candy until she'd finished nearly half of it. With care, she rewrapped the candy and placed it in her purse. A second later, she rose.

"I should be leaving," she said.

"Are you sure?"

Genevieve nodded and grasped her purse to her chest. "Yes," she said. "I've got to work tomorrow."

So did Ernest, but showing up at the sawmill was the last

thing on his mind. He climbed to his feet and tossed the candy wrapper in the trash bin.

"Then let's get you home before you turn into a pumpkin, Cinderella." He paused. "Which way do we go?"

"What do you mean?" Genevieve froze then pointed to the south. "The five-and-dime is that way."

He nodded. "Well, of course it is, but a gentleman wouldn't allow a lady to walk home alone. I'd feel much better if I could see you to your door."

"No."

Even though shadows hid part of her face, Ernest could see that Genevieve meant business. "Have it your way," he said as he offered her his arm. "But I don't like it one bit."

"Thank you," she said.

As they neared the five-and-dime, Ernest found his steps were a bit slower even as his heart raced. Just like yesterday at the soda counter, he didn't want their time together to end.

They arrived at the five-and-dime, now dark and empty. Ernest knew a gentleman would say a quick good-bye and make a hasty exit. At this moment, he had no interest in doing either. So without braving a look in Genevieve's direction, he plopped down on the third step and made himself at home.

An uncomfortable silence fell between them as Genevieve clutched the purse to her chest. Ernest searched his foggy brain for a topic they could chew on a bit. Ah, yes, Latanier. Talking about the bayou could eat up an unlimited amount of time.

෴

"So," he said casually, "have you been home lately?"

"To Latanier?" Genevieve shook her head then fumbled with the clasp on her purse. Home was the one place she longed to be and talking about it just hurt her heart. "No, not in a few weeks," she said as she cast about for a change of topic.

"You sound like you miss it."

Her startled gaze must have surprised him. "I do?"

"Well, sort of," he said. "But then, I understand, what with losing your papa and your mama being there by herself. Must be difficult."

"Yes, it is." She affected a casual pose. "I suppose you just miss home, too, what with the little ones changing so fast. It must seem like forever when you're away."

He gave her a strange look. "Actually, I do miss some of the things at home, but crying babies isn't one of them. Of course, now that the girls are older, it's not so bad."

If he'd waited on her for conversation, he would have had a long wait. Thankfully he interpreted her dumbstruck expression as a need for more information.

"You see, Eileen was barely toddling and Mary was a newborn when I took off for greener—and quieter—pastures," he said. "Now that they're three and four, I'm getting used to them; but I'll tell you, if I never hear another crying baby, it will be too soon."

"You don't like babies?" Gen tried to keep any sign of emotion from her voice. Whether she succeeded or not, she couldn't say. Her heart was pounding too hard to hear.

"Oh, sure, I love babies, as long as they don't live at my house or cry when I'm trying to think." He shrugged. "Anyway, I'm heading home tomorrow for my sister's birthday party. I'd be honored to meet you after work and take you with me."

Amidst the turmoil in her heart, she struggled to follow his change of topic. She was having a hard enough time accepting the fact that the man she'd become fond of had an aversion to babies.

"Home?" she muttered. "To Latanier?"

"Yes," he said, clearly puzzled, "to Latanier."

Gen shook her head. "I'm sorry, but that's not possible."

Ernest patted the step beside him. "All right, then, why don't you just sit a spell before we part company?" He grinned. "I promise I won't bite."

Gen realized she could either join him on the step or head home. There was danger in both, but allowing him to follow her seemed a bit more risky than sitting beside him until she could convince him to leave.

So without comment, she perched on the bottom step and tucked the hem of her dress around her ankles. The air had become brisk, with a slight breeze. Gen removed the sweater from her shoulders and put it on. If she couldn't be comfortable, at least she wouldn't be cold.

"Where were we? Ah, yes, we were talking about Latanier." He peered down at her intently. "I've noticed you don't use the Acadian language."

"No," she said slowly. "I don't suppose I do."

"Do you speak it. . . ?" He paused. "At all, I mean?"

"I used to," Gen said slowly. "Daddy thought it important that I learn the language of the people. He and I spoke to one another almost exclusively in Acadian French."

"What about your mother? Does she?"

"I suppose she still remembers it, although it used to be quite a game of mine to try and get her to speak or comment in it. Daddy insisted she could understand us, but I never could get her to prove him right. She didn't much like to hear it."

"Wonder why," he said.

Gen shrugged. "My father said it was because people thought the Acadians were backward. If you didn't speak English, you were somehow less, oh, I don't know."

Ernest nodded. "I know a lot of folks feel that way. Me personally, I don't, but then I also don't use the language much here in New Iberia. Now if I'm at home in Latanier, that's a whole other story."

"It's hard for me to hear it, even though I hear it all the time at the store." She looked away. "Reminds me too much of Daddy, I guess."

As she spoke her father's name, tears burned her eyes; tears for Daddy, for Mother, and for Ellen, but also for herself and the way she'd let both her earthly father and her heavenly Father down.

Determined not to let Ernest Breaux see her cry, Gen looked away and pretended to study something across the street. In truth, she could see nothing but a big blurry patch of grass where she knew the park should be. Someday, maybe, she'd swallow her pride and get those eyeglasses she ought to have.

But she would have to think of mundane things like eyeglasses later. For now, it was all she could do not to let the tears spill.

Ernest scooted down to sit beside her. Without a word, he took her hand in his.

How long they sat in silence, fingers entwined, Gen couldn't say. Finally, she gathered her wits and her purse and rose.

"Thank you for tonight," she said. "I had a good time."

"I'm glad to hear it." Ernest stretched his long legs then stood. "Now, about that trip to Latanier this weekend."

The thought of seeing her precious Ellen tempted her, but she'd been offered rare overtime hours tomorrow, and with their funds dwindling at an alarming rate and the taxes on the home place coming due, she had to accept the extra work. Still, her heart broke as she forced herself to turn Ernest's offer down.

"Well, then," he said slowly, "if you change your mind, let me know."

"Sure," she said, although she doubted any such thing would happen.

"All right, then. Oh, and before I forget, thank you for the candy. I can honestly say that was the best Milky Way bar a girl's ever bought for me." He grinned. "Course, it's the only Milky Way bar a girl's ever bought for me."

"Oh, hush." Gen gave Ernest a playful shove, and he caught her wrist with his hand.

Time suspended between silly play and serious emotions. Gen looked up into Ernest's eyes. The moment her gaze collided with his, he released his grip.

"I'm asking one more time if I can see you home, Genevieve," he said, his voice husky.

She paused to give the idea some thought. "Not this time, Ernest," she finally said. "Maybe some other time, but not tonight."

Ernest stared at her a moment longer then gave her a curt nod. "I'm a man of my word," he said, "so I'm going to turn my back to the street and let you head on home." He captured her hand in a firm grip, then shook it and let it go. "Good night, Genevieve Lamont."

"Good night, Ernest Breaux," she said as she took a step back.

He began to turn away from the street, then stopped and glanced over his shoulder. "I made you a promise; now I want one from you in return."

"What's that?"

"How loud can you scream?"

She shrugged. "I don't know. I guess I'm not all that loud. Why?"

"Can you whistle?"

"I was raised on a farm," she said with a grin. "Of course, I can."

"Show me," he said.

Gen let out her best whistle, the one she'd learned at her daddy's knee. Ernest looked suitably impressed.

So did the elderly man who lived above the five-and-dime. "You kids hush that racket down there," the old man called. "Don't you know it's nigh on ten o'clock?"

"Sorry, Mr. Prejean," Gen called. "We were just leaving."

"See that you make it snappy. A body needs to sleep, you know." The old man completed his response by slamming his window shut. Still, Gen could see him peering through half-open curtains.

"Well, now," Ernest said, "that was quite good."

"Thank you." She gave him a sideways look. "As Mr. Prejean said, it's nigh on ten o'clock. I should be going."

"Wait, you owe me a promise." Before she could comment, he held up his hand to silence her. "I only ask that if you're in trouble on the way home, you whistle. I'll come running. Would you promise me that?"

"I whistle, and you come running?" Gen grinned. "Now how could I say no to that?"

They shook on the bargain, and then Gen set off toward the boardinghouse. More than once, she stopped to make sure Ernest kept his promise. Each time she found him standing with his back to her.

As she turned the corner and Ernest Breaux disappeared from sight, it was all she could do not to whistle.

twelve

Saturday, May 13

Ernest lay on his back on the banks of Bayou Nouvelle, the warm sunshine making him feel as lazy as Papa's old hound dog. Not that he'd actually found the time to be lazy. Since he arrived, he'd been busy repairing benches and bracing tables, fixing the porch swing, and making a nice pile of wood shavings while carving new legs for Mama's rocker.

If he didn't know better, he'd think Papa left those jobs undone on purpose so he could praise Ernest when he completed them. Ernest had certainly heard enough comment about his carpentering skills to last a lifetime.

Yet he never got tired of the work.

What if Papa were right? What if the Lord did intend him to be a woodworker and not a sawmill employee?

Lord, if You intend it, You're going to have to show me how to manage it.

Through half-closed eyes, he watched Joseph and John splash in the shallows a few feet away. Each held a cane pole Ernest had fashioned to fit them, and they played at catching trophy-sized fish. Neither seemed to notice the lack of a line or hook.

Or for that matter, the fish. There were none in this part of the bayou. The water was far too black to support the fresh-water fish that thrived elsewhere.

"Mama's baking us a cake," John said as he pretended to cast toward the far side of the bayou.

Joseph might be younger than his twin by a full five minutes, but he lost nothing in a contest for attention. "Is not." He pointed his pole in the opposite direction and went through

96

the motions of casting his imaginary line. "She's baking the cake for Amalie. We only get to have some on account of it's her birthday today and not ours."

"That's right, and don't you forget it." Amalie strolled toward them with a smile.

Ernest propped himself up on his elbows and watched his sister approach. Long hair hung over one shoulder in a tight braid, and her apron looked starched and spotless, a sure sign she'd been hiding somewhere reading rather than helping Mama with the chores.

At the age of thirteen as of a quarter to ten this morning, she wore her beauty as if she had no idea of it. Slender as a reed and nearly as tall as Ernest, she seemed at one moment a child and the next a woman.

This fact made Ernest want to show her off and hide her away all at the same time. Papa mentioned last night that the bayou boys were beginning to line up on the doorstep to vie for her attention. In a few years she'd be married off like Angeline and Mathilde. Then where would he be?

Most likely fashioning another crib for the endless stream of babies the old home place had entertained over the years.

Amalie settled beside him and smoothed her skirts around her ankles. The action reminded him of Genevieve and their conversation on the steps of the five-and-dime Thursday night. At the thought of the lovely Miss Lamont, he began to whistle.

Ernest also began to wonder if Genevieve had changed her mind about traveling to Latanier this weekend. Maybe tomorrow after church he'd stop by her mama's place just to see if she was there.

His sister's chattering caught his notice. Ernest forced his mind back on Amalie. "What's that, cher?"

"I said that it's about time a girl got some attention around here, what with all these boys running around." Amalie shook her head. "Except for Eileen and Mary, even the babies are boys. Just last Sunday at church, the pastor's wife looked at Angeline and declared she would have another boy." She fisted her hands and hit her knees. "Another boy. Can you believe it?"

"I suppose," he said, "although I honestly don't see what the trouble is with boys. Someday you'll appreciate male attention, and it will be Papa or your brothers who say c'est tout. Enough."

As soon as he said the words, he wished he could reel them back in. No sense in stirring that pot until the stew was ready.

"Non, merci. I don't have time for that nonsense," she said with a wave of her hand. "Someday I'm going to write fabulous books that are turned into incredible movies that I will star in myself."

Ernest chuckled. "Now that's a lofty dream."

"Well, it might be, but God gave that dream to me, and the Bible says there's nothing God can't do. Until He changes His mind about my destiny, I'm not changing mine." She shrugged. "Anyway, just promise me that you will give Mama and Papa lots of granddaughters. Do you hear me? Girls, Ernest. This family needs more women."

Amalie turned that last statement into the height of drama. She even pretended to swoon.

Whistling turned to laughter. "Mais non, but you do say the most outrageous things, cher. What makes you think I plan to give Mama and Papa any grandbabies?"

"I'm young, but I'm not that young," she said, giving him a sideways glance. "I hear things."

He turned his face to the sun and closed his eyes. This should be good. Much of what Amalie claimed to hear turned out to be the fruit of her active imagination.

"Oh?" Ernest said as the sun's warmth continued to lull him into laziness. "Like what?"

"Like you've been spending time with Genevieve Lamont. Like you're sweet on her."

Ernest sat bolt upright and opened his eyes, blinding himself in the process. "Who told you that?" he asked as he tried to blink the world back into focus.

"Like I said, I hear things." She reached for a blade of grass and studied it. "People talk, Ernest, and most times they figure a girl with a book in her hand isn't listening."

The topic of Genevieve needed to be handled with care, this much Ernest knew. If his sister got wind of the fact that he truly had given some thought to developing a more serious relationship with Miss Lamont, Amalie would never let him hear the end of it.

The one thing that girl loved more than a good book or movie was a good family drama. And of course, he and his siblings were generally the stars of the story.

He gave his sister a sideways glance and decided humor was the only way to handle her.

"I'm sorry, what did you say? I wasn't listening."

She gave Ernest a playful shove, then looked toward the bayou. John and Joseph had left their poles on the bank and were now chasing turtles. "You boys get back on dry land, you hear? Mama's going to be calling us all to supper soon."

John obeyed immediately while Joseph tarried. "Do as your sister says, Joseph," Ernest called. "And don't make me come in after you."

Well, that was obviously an invitation to disobey if ever Joseph heard one. He giggled then disappeared under the water. A second later he rose from the murky stream, his hair wet and black as a seal and rivulets of water running off his outstretched hands.

"Look, Ernest, I'm a big old fish. I betcha won't come and catch me."

"Look at me, Ernest," John called as he dove in after his twin. "I'm a fish, too. A big old fat fish with smelly scales and things on the side of my face that go like this." He emerged from the water with his hands beside his ears in a rough imitation of gills.

"Boys," Amalie said with a groan.

"That's right, Amalie. You'd do better to stick to your books and your movies." Ernest chuckled and climbed to his feet.

"You'd better go on home and tell Mama her boys turned into bayou fishes." He paused to wink at the twins. "Even the oldest."

"Oh, no," she said. "Ernest, you're not getting in the water with them, are you?"

"There was a time, Mademoiselle Amalie, when you loved nothing better than a swim in the bayou. What happened?"

She looked at him with disdain. "I grew up."

"Well, not me." Ernest kicked off his shoes and began to roll his pant legs up. Before he could prepare himself to wade in the shallows, Joseph had climbed on his back. John grabbed him around the waist, and together the three of them fell into the water.

Ernest came up sputtering, his brothers swimming in circles around him like the fish they claimed to be.

Amalie stood at the bank, keeping a healthy distance between herself and the reach of their splashes. "Oh, I'll be telling Mama, all right," she said. "I'm telling her that what I just saw proves my theory that there are too many men around here. They get together and their brains shrink up to nothing."

"Oh, please don't do that. Here, you can come swimming with us." Ernest pretended to chase her. "Come on back, birthday girl. Don't you want to have a birthday swim with us?"

Ernest watched Amalie hightail it down the path leading away from the bayou. In short order, she'd reach home, and depending on which one she saw first, she'd either rat him out to Mama or to Papa. By the time the three of them arrived on the front porch, there would be a less-than-happy set of parents waiting for them.

He knew it as well as he knew his name. Yet something made him linger just a bit longer in the black water.

It might have been the fun he had teasing his brothers and pretending to chase them in the shallows. It could have been the way he loved letting the twins climb on his back while he swam laps beneath the weeping willow. Or maybe it was the fact that he hadn't laughed so hard since his date with Genevieve on Thursday night.

Laughing was good for him, he decided. And so was playing with the twins.

Then he spied Mama heading down the path toward them. "Ernest Theophile Alfred Breaux, is that you I see acting the fool as wet as a duck in the bayou?"

Ernest knelt down and grabbed the twins, positioning them in front of him. "Quick, boys, hide me. I think Mama's gonna take the belt to me for getting wet so close to supper. Don't tell her where I am."

"Boys, where's your brother?" Mama called.

A giggling Joseph and John pointed behind them. "Right here, Mama," they said in unison.

"Thanks a lot, you turncoats. One question from Mama and you're squawking like a jaybird." Ernest stood and hefted a squealing boy onto each shoulder. "They made me, Mama. I didn't want to get wet."

"We did not," echoed two similar yet distinct childish voices.

"Put them down, Ernest Breaux." Mama stood with her hands on her hips, obviously trying to keep a straight face. "Joseph and John, I sent you out here to keep your brother company. Do you think you ought to be swimming when you're supposed to be watching Ernest?"

She pretended to swat their bottoms as they raced past. Each one scooted out of her reach in time for her hand to hit air, a familiar ploy with Breaux children. Mama had never actually spanked a one of them, but she'd made the attempt many times over.

With the wisdom of adulthood, Ernest was left to wonder whether Mama let them think they were getting away with something or not. Surely she would have made contact with one of them along the way if she'd intended to.

Ernest swung his arms around Mama and picked her up as he hugged her. She cried out in protest at the wet embrace, all the while giggling.

"Ernest Breaux, you are as bad as your papa," she said as

she smoothed her apron and brushed away the water from her shoulders. "What am I going to do with you?"

He bowed from the waist and smiled. "Why, thank you, Mama. You've paid me a high compliment."

"Oh, hush," she said as she turned toward the house. "You are just the end, son. Now come on back home and get into dry clothes. Supper's almost on the table, and I want everything to be special for Amalie."

"You're special, Mama. Don't you know that?"

Ernest caught her and swung her into his arms. Once again, she squealed in protest. Finally he let her down.

"If you do that one more time, I am going to whack the tar out of you, Ernest," she said. "Just because you've been taller than me since you turned ten, that doesn't mean I ought to be thrown about like a rag doll; yet every time you get a chance, you do just that. You got some problem that you don't understand that I like my feet on the ground, son?"

Ernest wrapped his arm around her waist and gave her a gentle hug. "I'm sorry, Mama," he said. "According to Amalie, my problem is that I'm a man."

Papa's laughter boomed. "Well, now, I don't see how being a man is a problem."

Ernest looked up to see his father and brothers sitting on the porch. Amalie stood in the doorway. "Ask Amalie, Papa. She'll explain it where even a man can understand."

"Oh, hush, son," Mama said. "Don't you go causing a fuss on your sister's birthday." She pointed to the staircase beside Papa, the one that led from the porch to the upstairs portion of the house where Ernest and his brothers slept. "Head on upstairs and change into something dry. I would like to have all of you at the supper table on time tonight."

"Yes, ma'am," he said as he gave Amalie a wink, then climbed the stairs. Ten minutes later he wore dry clothes and had his hair slicked back away from his face the way Mama liked it. Mama didn't take any more kindly to hats in the house than she did to shaggy hair, so he left his cap upstairs atop his suitcase.

As he descended the stairs, Amalie's birthday present tucked in the crook of his arm, he smiled. Thanks to Genevieve Lamont, his sister would be pleased with his gift.

The fact that Amalie had heard talk of their friendship troubled Ernest. Why the bayou women had nothing better to do than speculate on his love life perplexed him.

After all, there was nothing to talk about.

"There's my oldest bebe," Mama called as he walked in.

He kissed the top of Mama's head, then set his gift on the table with the others. "Mama, when are you going to stop calling me your baby? I am pushing thirty, you know."

"You're twenty-eight, Ernest," his sister Angeline said. "Don't rush thirty. I'm too close to you in age."

Ernest gave his heavily pregnant sister a kiss on the cheek, then allowed her toddling son to climb into his outstretched arms. "I can't help that time marches on, Angeline. Why, before you know it, this bruiser's going to have children of his own."

He tickled his nephew's chubby belly then tossed him into the air and caught him. All the while, the little boy giggled, arms flailing. When Ernest handed him back to his father, he whirled around to find a line of nephews and brothers had formed, each vying for his attention.

"Oh, no, you don't," he said to the assembled group. "If I start this with all of you, we will never get supper."

"That's right," Amalie said as she took her place of honor at the table. "And whoever isn't washed up for supper when Papa sits down doesn't get any birthday cake."

Little Joseph peered up at Ernest, his hair still wet and slicked back from his swim. "Is that right, Ernest?"

He pretended to give the matter great thought. "Oui," he said. "That's the truth. You all better hurry outside to wash before Papa decides he wants to stand up and amble over to the table."

Papa stretched his long legs and yawned. "I am a mite tired from working the traps this afternoon. I believe my belly's complaining, too. That supper of yours almost ready, Mama?"

"It is," Mama called. "Just go ahead and set yourself at the table, Papa."

With that, the room cleared of all bodies under the age of twelve. Mama and Papa exchanged a chuckle.

"I declare, Ernest," his sister Mathilde said as she placed the gumbo pot at the center of the long table. "You are the Pied Piper of babies and little children. They all love you."

"That's right," her husband, Nicolas Arceneaux, said. "When do you intend to settle down and have a few of your own?"

"A few?" Papa said with a snort. "I told him long ago he ought to have a houseful. Babies keep a body young and a household happy."

Angeline patted her belly. "I don't know about keeping you young, Papa. Today I feel as old as the hills."

Mama shook her head as she wiped her hands on her apron. "This too shall pass. You just wait until your babies are this size." She gestured toward Ernest. "Then you'll appreciate them. Why, just look at those table legs. See this." She placed her hands on the table and gave it a shove. "It used to rock so bad we had to put folded paper under there. But Ernest, he built me all new legs for it. Now it sits just fine. *Merci beaucoup*, son."

Ernest shrugged. "It was nothing, Mama."

Papa nudged Ernest. "Maybe nothing to you, but a man who knows good work like me, well, I say it was something. You give any more thought to turning that talent of yours into a business, eh?"

"No, honestly I haven't, Papa." He sighed. "But I have been doing a little puttering around in the wood shop at work after hours. I've got some plans for a dining room set out in the car. If you'd like, I can show them to you after the party."

He smiled. "I'd like that a lot, son. Oh, and while we're out there, what say you and me take a drive, eh?"

"I'd love to, Papa," Ernest said.

"Good." Papa rose and clapped a hand on Ernest's shoulder. "I did enjoy driving your motorcar the last time you were here."

thirteen

Dinner came and went, and Ernest ate more gumbo than he thought possible. The first bowl disappeared well before the growling in his belly ceased, and the second didn't fill the empty spot he still felt. Finally, after consuming his third bowl, he decided he'd had enough.

While Mathilde brewed coffee and Mama cut slices of cake, Amalie began to open her gifts. As she reached for Ernest's package, he turned to watch.

He'd wrapped the gift himself, using the materials he had on hand: glue, string, and the Sunday edition of the newspaper. It took her a little longer than he expected to unwrap the gift, but when she'd finally loosened the paper, she let out a squeal of delight.

"Oh, Ernest, it's Nancy Drew!" Amalie climbed over Eileen and Mary, who were playing with the gift's torn wrappings, to give Ernest a hug. "I love these books. How did you know?"

He shrugged. "A little bird told me."

Amalie gave him a sideways look and leaned close to whisper in his ear. "A little bird or a girl named Genevieve?"

"I'm going to ignore that."

Thankfully, Amalie was too busy to comment further. An hour later, the party had moved outside, as had the noise. Those children whose mothers hadn't sent them to bed were taking the rare opportunity to whoop it up and run about in the dark.

To Ernest's thinking, it looked like fun. He felt sorely tempted to join them rather than sit with the adults and sip coffee and talk about politics and the weather.

Ernest leaned back from the table and pushed his plate away. As always, Mama's cake was delicious. He glanced over to tell her so when he caught her staring.

"What?" he asked. "You look like something's bothering you."

She shook her head then paused to nod. "I'd like to talk to you, bebe," she whispered.

"Sure." Ernest rose. "If you all will excuse us, I'm going to take a walk with my best girl." He offered his mother his hand. "Mama, shall we?"

A few minutes later, the pair had traversed the lawn and, to the dismay of the children, turned to walk alone down the path heading toward the bayou. Ernest slowed his stride to keep pace with his mother, all the while inhaling the fresh night air.

"It don't smell like this in the city, does it?" Mama asked.

Ernest held up a low branch so that Mama could walk beneath it. "No, Mama."

"But I didn't bring you out here to talk about that." She stopped beneath a circle of moonlight and crossed her arms over her chest. "You are my firstborn, Ernest, the bebe I prayed for before I ever met your papa. Did I ever tell you that when I would daydream, I would imagine a family with a boy and a girl? And that boy, I would name him Ernest."

"No, I didn't know that."

"It just seems like I've always known about you." She paused. "I'm rambling, aren't I?"

Ernest wrapped his arm around her waist and looked down on Mama with a smile. "You're doing fine."

Mama nodded. "Well, then, that's all well and good, but I need to get to the point. I'm just gonna tell it to you straight."

"That'd be fine by me." He gestured to the bench he'd made some ten years ago, now used as a thinking spot for Papa. "Allons. Why don't we sit down?"

"You go on and sit. That way I can look you in the eye." After Ernest complied, Mama regarded him with a steady gaze. "There's been talk, son. They say you've taken up with Genevieve Lamont. I'm asking you if it's so."

"They?"

Her look dared him to try and deflect the question. "Don't ask me who's been talking; just tell me if it's the truth."

Ernest chewed on a couple of possible answers. Ultimately he went for the simplest and most truthful. "Not yet."

Mama settled beside him. "What do you mean by that?"

What did he mean? He sighed. "I suppose I'm saying that I've gone on one date, Mama. I like her, and maybe she likes me. Maybe she doesn't. I don't know."

He paused and hoped Mama would take her turn at talking so he wouldn't have to continue. Unfortunately, she didn't.

"She's real nice." Another pause, this one to consider just how to make his next point. "And she's pretty, Mama, real pretty. But you know what else?"

"Qui c'est sa?"

He leaned against the back of the bench and stared up into the night sky. "She makes me laugh. And more than that, when I think about her two or three days later, it still puts a smile on my face."

Mama took his hand in hers and squeezed. "Oh, son, that sounds serious."

Ernest shrugged. *"Pas du tout.* Not hardly, Mama. She's just someone I enjoy spending time with."

"Maybe." Another squeeze and she released her grip. "Just promise me one thing, Ernest."

He swiveled to meet her gaze. "What's that?"

"Promise that no matter what happens, you won't judge." She looked away. "Things are not always as they appear, you know."

She looked so serious that he hated to chuckle. "Mama, I don't know what you're talking about. Why would you say something like that?"

"Just promise it, Ernest."

"Sure," he said. "I promise, although I have no idea why you would think I need to."

Mama shook her head. "Honey, all I'm saying is that I don't want you to miss out on your chance for love because you made up your mind before you knew the Lord's take on things. You hear?"

"Hold on here, Mama. No one said anything about love."

His mother smiled. "No one had to."

Sunday, May 14

The preaching was fine and so was Sunday lunch, but impatience kept tugging Ernest toward the open door and the motorcar parked outside. When he finally managed to set off down the road to New Iberia, it didn't take him long to find the roadster pointed toward the Lamont place.

Ernest slowed to make the turn onto the long dirt road leading to the house, then pulled over and stopped. In the distance, the white, two-story home loomed on a high spot near the bayou. Unlike the other homes in the area, this one did not bear any of the traditional Acadian features. Rather than leave the cypress boards unpainted, Mr. Lamont had them whitewashed, and instead of building his staircase outside to bypass the tax laws, he had centered his in the middle of the house. The result was a home that looked like it belonged in the city rather than set out amongst the weeping willows and bald cypress.

He shaded his eyes with his hand and peered across the distance. There seemed to be no one about.

For a moment, he considered turning tail and running. Then he thought about the possibility that Genevieve Lamont might be sitting somewhere inside that white house in need of a ride back to New Iberia.

It was that thought that caused him to climb back into the roadster and crank the engine. Easing the car over the ruts, he bounced toward the big house. As he neared the clearing, he noticed a thin plume of smoke coming from the chimney of the little wood frame house just beyond the summer kitchen.

It was the overseer's place—Ernest remembered that much. He also remembered the tales that were told about the man who had lived there, a man who had been killed in a way that no one wanted to describe to children.

So, as children often do, Ernest and his friends made up stories on the schoolyard about what happened to the poor fellow. Years later when he heard the true tale, he realized he'd never have understood the idea of hating a man for the color of his skin as a child.

Even now it bore hard on him.

The roadster rolled on toward the white house on the hill, and Ernest forced his thoughts back to Genevieve. Should he call her name or possibly honk the horn to announce his arrival? Maybe he ought to climb out and go to the door like a proper gentleman.

That last option appealed the most, so he did just that. Throwing his leg over the door, he jumped out of the car and straightened his cap. Satisfied he'd done the best he could to look presentable, Ernest strode to the door and knocked twice.

No answer.

He tried again, giving the old door three solid whacks with his fist. "Miss Lamont?" he called. "You home?"

Again, nothing.

Ernest stepped back and stared hard at the door, willing it to open. Once more he tried knocking. He also called Genevieve's name.

"Allons! You there, Monsieur Breaux."

Whirling around, he saw a large dark woman coming up the path carrying a bawling infant. A mongrel dog circled them, making quite a ruckus with his barks and yips. The trio made their way toward him, a noisy symphony that made him want to get on his knees right there and thank the Lord he had neither child nor dog back home in New Iberia.

"Monsieur Breaux, I'm Big Mama," the woman called again. *"Comment ça va?"*

"Ça va bien," Ernest answered. The proper Acadian greetings out of the way, Ernest went straight to the point. "Mademoiselle Lamont, is she here?"

"Mais non," the woman said, shouting to be heard over the baby and dog. "Nobody's t'home. They all gone."

She brushed past Ernest to stand between him and the door. "Hush," she shouted to the dog. The command worked, both with the mangy animal and the dark-haired baby. While the dog slunk away to lie in the shade of a magnolia, the baby stared at him, lower lip quivering.

The little one couldn't have been more than six months old and, judging from the pink clothing, must be a girl. Big eyes the color of chicory coffee stared up at him, dark lashes wet with tears.

"What's wrong, sweetheart?" he asked, giving the wet-faced girl a smile.

She blinked hard then looked up at the dark woman who held her. Finally she stared back at Ernest.

Then she grinned.

"Well, now, would you look at that?" the woman said. "I don't believe I've ever seen her take to a stranger like that."

Before he could comment, the child burst into tears again. Her wail pierced Ernest's eardrums and made him want to run for the roadster. Only the prospect of finding Genevieve Lamont kept him rooted in place.

"You said the Lamonts are not home," he shouted. "Can you tell me when they will return?"

" 'Fraid not," she said as she reached for the door. "Miss Genevieve, she don't live here no more, and her mama, well, that's not who you came to see, is it?"

Ernest shook his head. The woman's stare unnerved him. Why, except for the obvious, she could have been Genevieve's mother the way she acted so protective. His attention went from the woman to the baby.

What a strange combination they were, these two. The calm-faced dark woman and the bawling pale child.

"If you'll excuse me, this 'un's hungry. Next time I see Miss Genny, I'll be sure an' tell her you was here. Oh, I won't forget that, no." She reached for the knob and gave it a yank.

"You take care now, you hear?"

Without further comment, she stepped inside and let the door close behind her, leaving Ernest standing on the porch alone. He took two steps back and waited, thinking the woman might reappear. After a few minutes, he realized she did not intend to.

Feeling the fool, Ernest beat a path back to the roadster and climbed inside. As he reached down to crank the engine, a flash of white in an upper window caught his attention. He sat up straight and stared.

In the top, right-hand window stood a woman wearing white. Upon closer inspection, he realized it was a white dressing gown over a pair of light-colored men's pajamas. Before he could react, the woman stepped back and disappeared into the shadows.

All the way back to New Iberia, Ernest debated whether he should tell Genevieve he'd stopped by her place. In the end, he decided he'd keep that fact to himself.

Unless she asked, of course.

fourteen

In his quest to win another date with Genevieve Lamont, Ernest managed to down an average of three sodas a day for a week. Finally, on the eighth day of his campaign, she said yes. This time, they would go for a drive rather than see a movie, something Ernest thought might give him time to learn more about the secretive Miss Lamont. To his surprise, Genevieve insisted on bringing a picnic dinner.

That evening, he picked up Genevieve and her hamper of food on the steps of the five-and-dime at a quarter past six. She had on the same green dress she'd worn on their last date, and it pleased him that she would remember he liked it. He was about to say so when she turned to him and smiled.

All words fled, and he became, well, speechless.

Somehow he managed to help her into the roadster, then run around to jump inside himself. He cranked the engine and turned to smile at his guest.

In this light with the sun teasing the tops of the trees, Genevieve Lamont looked absolutely stunning. There she sat, wearing not a drop of makeup and with her hair caught up in an old-fashioned coil at the nape of her neck, yet he'd never seen a woman look more beautiful.

"I hope you like chicken and potato salad. Oh, and biscuits." She pointed to the hamper at her feet. "That's what I brought." The object of his attention frowned. "What's wrong?"

"Wrong? Oh, nothing," he said quickly as he turned his attention to putting the car into gear.

As he stopped the car at the first stop sign, he saw her reach for her purse, then pull out a flowered scarf to cover her hair. "To protect it from the wind," she said as she leaned back in the seat.

Ernest nodded. A horn honked, and he jumped then pressed the accelerator. Until he could get safely out of New Iberia, he could not afford to pay any further attention to his passenger.

The results might be dangerous.

Soon the roadster was flying down a deserted country road. With the sun at his back and Genevieve at his side, Ernest could have driven until the gas ran out, except that his stomach complained. He pulled over next to a green field beside the bayou and turned off the car.

"How's this?"

Genevieve smiled and gathered up the hamper. "Perfect," she said as she climbed out.

A few minutes later, they sat on a blanket with plates of fried chicken and potato salad. Ernest took a bite and groaned. "If you cooked this chicken, I think I'm in love."

He froze. *Oh, no, did I say that out loud?*

Her shocked expression was followed by a grin. "Well, then," she said as she handed him a fork, "I guess you're out with the wrong girl."

"Oh," Ernest said. "How's that?"

She giggled. "My roommate, Betty, made the chicken."

"Get the recipe," he said as he stabbed his fork into the potato salad and took a healthy bite. "Now this is good eating."

"Thanks. It's a family recipe."

He leaned toward her. "I think I like your family."

She met him halfway. "Oh, really?"

They were almost nose to nose. Before he could do what his heart demanded and kiss her, he listened to his head and reached for another piece of chicken. He watched her out of the corner of his eye as he chewed. Was that relief he saw on her face or disappointment?

His pride hoped for the latter.

By the time he finished his meal, Ernest decided it was time to come clean about his visit to the Lamont place. He was about to say something when Genevieve began to speak.

"Ernest, I understand you paid Mother's housekeeper a visit."

He tried to read the expression on her face. "Yes, actually," he finally said. "I thought maybe you'd changed your mind about Latanier. I wanted to offer a ride back to New Iberia."

"I wondered why you did that." She began to pack the empty plates. "And I also wondered why you didn't mention anything about it."

"Well, actually, I was about to." Ernest shrugged. "I know the timing seems questionable, but I promise I was going to tell you. I mean, I assume you spoke to the housekeeper."

Genevieve wrapped the last of the chicken in a towel and set it atop the plates. "Yes."

"Well, ever since then I wondered how your mother was doing."

The color drained out of her face. "My mother?"

"Yes, I saw her standing in the window. I assumed, because she was in her nightclothes and all, that she might be ill. I couldn't hardly ask how she was doing without letting you know I was there, now could I?" He paused. "And that baby, I wondered about her. She surely didn't belong to the housekeeper. That much was obvious."

"You saw a baby there? I wasn't told this."

Ernest nodded. "Little girl about so big." He indicated the baby's size with his hands. "Had a healthy set of lungs on her, that's for sure."

Genevieve closed the lid on the hamper and gave him a direct look. This time there was no mistaking her feelings. She was not happy.

"I don't know if you've realized this about me, but I'm a very private person."

"Yes," he said. "I've noticed. What's your point?"

"Ernest, I like you." She sighed. "Actually, I like you a lot."

He leaned toward her and reached for her hand. To his surprise, she let him wrap his fingers around hers. "I like you, too, Genevieve."

"Then will you just do one thing for me?"

"Anything."

Genevieve pulled away and stood. "Would you take me home?"

Ernest scrambled to his feet and grasped her wrist. "What's wrong? Don't you feel well?"

She shook her head and he let her go. "I'm fine. It's just that. . .well, never mind."

Tears glistened, and she turned her head. Reaching for the hamper, she lifted it into the car, then yanked on the door latch.

"Wait." He pulled her into an embrace. "Don't cry. Whatever I've done, I'm sorry."

She rested her forehead on his chest and, an eternity later, looked up into his eyes. "Ernest, you have no idea what you've done."

"No," he said slowly, "I don't. But I know it upset you, and that's the last thing I ever wanted to do."

Brown eyes continued to stare up at him. A gentleman would have released her to offer her his handkerchief. Instead, he kissed her.

It was a soft kiss, one of those sweet, brief meetings of the lips that held much promise and no disappointment.

Their fist kiss and it tasted of salty tears. *Lord, please let this be the last time I make her cry.*

"Do you still want me to take you home?" he whispered into her ear.

"Yes," she said in a small voice, and then she added, "Please."

Reluctant to break the embrace, he let her pull away first. When she did, he helped her into the car, then folded the blanket and tucked it behind the hamper. Finally he climbed in and cranked the engine.

"Ernest?"

He gave her a sideways look. "Yes?"

"Would you do that one more time?"

"Do what?"

She leaned over to place her hand atop his. "Would you kiss me? Just once more."

He adjusted his cap with his free hand and pretended to consider the question. "Will you let me take you home instead of back to the five-and-dime?" he finally asked.

"No," she said softly. "Does that make a difference?"

"No, but next time we go out on a date. . ." Ernest leaned toward her, stopping inches from her lips. "I will take you home"—he moved a hairbreadth closer—"to your door." He paused. "Is that understood?"

Genevieve answered with a nearly breathless, "Yes."

જ

Wednesday, May 24

The next morning, Ernest rose with a smile remembering the three kisses he had bestowed on the lovely Miss Lamont. Besides the two on the picnic, he'd received one more kiss before he left her off on the steps of the five-and-dime. On top of that, they had a date for tomorrow night, this time to the movies.

His feet touched the ground, barely, as he arrived at work. Before he could take his position on the line, Mr. Denison's secretary came to fetch him. He was needed, it seemed, in the sawmill owner's private office.

Ernest knocked twice and was let in by the boss himself. "Come on in, son, and have a seat."

Mr. Denison gestured to a leather chair Ernest knew well. He'd repaired the arm on it just last week in his spare time. He did as he was told then watched his boss settle on the other side of a massive desk cluttered with papers and drawings. It was all he could do not to groan aloud when he noticed the drawing on top was his, a set of plans for a dining table he'd been playing around with. He must have left it on the sawmill floor after work yesterday.

Understandable since all he had on his mind was his impending date with Genevieve.

"Would you like some coffee?"

"What? Oh, no, thank you, Mr. Denison. I just had a cup at home."

Mr. Denison nodded. "Then I'll get right to the point." He leaned forward. "Ernest, I've been watching you. You're a right fine employee. Always early to work and never missed a day in three years. That's impressive."

Ernest said nothing.

"Yes, well, one of the fellows on the night shift brought this to my attention." He fished out the drawing and thrust it toward Ernest. "Did you do this?"

He could lie and possibly keep himself employed. Instead, he told the truth. "Yes, sir, I did. I'd like to tell you I owe you an apology for doing that on company time. It's just that the machines were down for maintenance, and the boys and I were standing around waiting. I found that piece of paper and decided to make good use of my time." He paused. "It won't happen again, I promise."

"It'd better happen again," Mr. Denison said. "Today, in fact."

Ernest shook his head. "I don't understand."

"Are you a carpenter, son? What I mean is, do you make these things or do you just draw them?"

"Both, sir," he said.

"Would you be willing to make something for me? If I paid you for it, I mean?"

"Sure," Ernest said. "I'd be glad to."

Mr. Denison grinned. "I've been trying to find the time to take my new bride shopping for a dining set. I'm afraid my bachelor apartment didn't have much more than the basics, and a dining table wasn't one of them." He shook the paper at Ernest. "Imagine how happy she will be when I tell her she can have anything she wants." He paused. "Within reason, of course."

"Of course."

He rose, and Ernest did the same. "I'll bring her back here after lunch, and the two of you can talk about what she's looking for. How's that?"

"That would be just fine." He shook hands with his boss, then walked back to the line with a grin.

That afternoon, he met the new Mrs. Denison and devised a set of drawings for a table and four chairs. By the time Ernest left work that evening, Mrs. Denison had sent word that she'd changed her mind and wanted six chairs and a longer table.

"You never know how many mouths the Lord will bless us to feed," she said by way of explanation.

After he'd escorted his wife out, Mr. Denison returned to follow Ernest out to the car, chatting with excitement. When he saw the roadster, he paused. "She looks like a million bucks, Ernest." He moved closer to inspect her. "What did you do to her?"

"Just a little work here and there."

He ran his hand over the fender and grinned. "Why, I'm almost tempted to buy her back."

"I believe you'll understand if I don't take you up on that, sir."

"Yes, I do." He paused. "About my wife's dining set. Have you given any thought to what sort of wood it ought to be made out of? I'm hoping we can find something here at the mill."

Ernest nodded. "Yes, sir, I believe we can. I noticed there's a nice pile of good quality ash over in the south corner of the warehouse. I believe there's enough to make quite a set."

"Yes," Mr. Denison said. "I know the lot you're talking about. That's expensive stuff, son."

"I agree," he said, "and there's plenty of red oak or cypress in stock to make an acceptable set." Ernest paused. "But then, I believe you would agree that your wife deserves the best. If she were to find that she'd been given cypress or oak when there was ash to be had, she might not be as happy with her purchase."

Mr. Denison studied him a moment then broke out in a grin. "You sure are a good judge of wood and women. I'm sure your wife is pleased with you."

Ernest wiped a speck of dust off the hood with the back of his shirt sleeve. "Thank you all the same, sir, but I don't have a wife, and I don't have any plans to acquire one."

His grin broadened. "Now isn't that always the way?"

"I don't understand."

"I didn't have plans to acquire a wife either. Told everyone who would listen I was a confirmed bachelor. The way I had it figured, I was meant to spend my time and money on the Lord's business." Mr. Denison leaned against the roadster and shook his head. "Funny, but somewhere between bachelorhood and fatherhood I realized that sometimes the Lord has other plans, and sometimes His business starts at your own front door. You see, I married a widow with a young son. So not only am I a husband now, I'm also a father."

Ernest whistled softly.

"Yep, that's my sentiments exactly, but you know what?"

"What's that, sir?"

Mr. Denison smiled. "That little fellow's not my son by birth, but it didn't take but about five minutes with him to start feeling like he's mine all the same. Now I'd welcome a dozen just like him."

Ernest chuckled. "Then, sir, I believe you're going to need a much longer table."

fifteen

As soon as Ernest said his good-byes to Mr. Denison and started the roadster, he pointed it toward the five-and-dime. Wouldn't Genevieve be surprised by his news?

He had to circle the block twice before he could find a place to park, but he finally managed it. By the time he turned off the engine and bounded across the street, he could hardly contain his smile.

A check of the clock on the square told him the time was half past four. Genevieve would be at work for another thirty minutes. Should he tell her immediately or buy a soda and wait until she finished for the day? Stepping inside, he looked for Genevieve. A search of the soda counter, the cash register, and even the book aisle turned up nothing.

"You looking for Genevieve?"

Ernest glanced up to see a familiar face standing at the end of the book aisle. "You're her friend, aren't you? Barbara?"

She nodded as she walked toward him. "That's right, but I'm Betty."

"Betty. Sorry. You're the one who made that delicious chicken, right?"

"That's me." Her smile faded. "Genevieve's not here today."

"She's not?" He shook his head. "Are you sure?"

"She's sure," Lester Bonfils said as he pressed past Betty. "Go on back to the register, hon. I'll handle this customer." He narrowed his eyes and stared at Ernest. "She called in sick today, and I suggest you tell her when you see her that I keep track of these things. That's twice in a month, sir. I've a good mind to fire her if she does it again."

"Have you considered that she might actually be ill, sir?"

Lester snorted and turned to walk away. "Not for a minute,"

he said. "Pretty ones like that girl don't last. They find a man and take off." He stopped to glance back at Ernest. "If you're the one she's latched onto, tell her if she can't get out of bed in time for work, she doesn't need to have a job." He chuckled. "But judging from the fact you're standing here with no idea where she is, I'd say you got thrown over for another fellow. Tough luck there, buddy."

Rather than punch the man, Ernest turned and stalked out of the five-and-dime. Before he could reach the roadster, he heard someone call his name. Betty caught up with him at the curb. Rather than speak, she pressed a piece of paper into his palm, then raced back toward the five-and-dime.

He opened the slip of paper and found an address. Five minutes later, he stood in front of the apartment listed on the page in front of him. He had to knock twice before anyone answered, but when the door swung open, there stood Genevieve Lamont.

She looked as if she hadn't slept, and the smile on her lips didn't quite make it to her eyes. Strange, but she didn't seem surprised to see him. Rather, she stepped out into the hall and closed the door behind her.

"I thought you might show up here," she said as she studied the faded roses on the carpet. "Leave it to Betty and her big mouth."

"I was worried about you." He placed his finger beneath her chin and lifted her gaze to meet his. "What's wrong?"

❧

"Wrong?"

Where to begin? She could give up her secrets and tell Ernest that she'd not slept more than an hour at a time since yesterday for worrying about her daughter. A call from Big Mama on the landlady's telephone last night informed her that Ellen was running a slight fever and had a nasty cough.

Gen knew that if Big Mama had taken the trouble of going next door to the Widow LeBlanc's house to borrow the telephone, the odds were that Ellen was much sicker than the woman had let on. Gen slept in fits and starts, forcing herself to lie down even though her instinct was to pace. When the sun rose over New Iberia, Gen was ready to head to the bus station. If only she had followed her first thought and headed home. She wouldn't be standing here trying to hide yet another secret from Ernest Breaux.

"Lester said you called in sick."

She nodded.

"But you don't look sick." He studied her a moment, then pressed his palm to her forehead. "No fever. And you're not sneezing. Actually, you just look tired. Did you have trouble sleeping last night?"

"Yes," she said softly. "I suppose you could say that."

"Any particular reason?"

Exhaustion fought with fear for supremacy, and the result was tears that first glistened then fell. Ernest took her into his arms and held her while she cried, standing silent and asking nothing of her except whether she needed his handkerchief.

Ultimately he gave her that handkerchief, even though she insisted she was fine. When she calmed a bit, she folded the handkerchief and attempted to hand it back to him. With a grin, he refused, saying she might need it later.

Gen ducked out of his embrace and leaned against the wall, the handkerchief clutched in her fist. "I should go back inside now. Maybe take a nap."

Ernest shook his head. "I wish you wouldn't. You don't need to be alone. Not when you're upset."

She looked up at him through tired eyes. "Betty will be home later. I'll be fine until then."

"Have you eaten anything today?"

She hadn't, but he didn't need to know that. "I'm fine, really, Ernest."

"Humor me, Genevieve. I'm worried about you." He laced his fingers with hers. "What if I bring you something? I can fetch something quick from Mulotte's and be back in ten minutes."

"No, really," she said. "Don't do that. My place isn't suitable to entertain men."

He looked to be at a loss, then he snapped his fingers. "I know. We'll have another picnic."

She must have looked doubtful because he upped the wattage on his smile. "It will be great, really. This time let me provide the food. I can't top your potato salad or Betty's chicken, but I bet I can grab a couple of sandwiches and be down at the park before you."

"Oh, I don't know." She clutched at the locket lying against her neck. "I'm afraid I wouldn't be much company."

He touched her chin with his thumb. "Sweetheart, I'm not asking you to be good company. I'm just asking you to show up. Would you do that for me? I'm worried."

What harm would it do to share a sandwich in the park with him? After all, despite the impression she gave him, Ernest Breaux had consumed her daily thoughts and nightly dreams ever since those kisses they shared.

"All right," she said slowly. "What if I meet you at the park in half an hour? Will that be all right?"

"Make it twenty minutes, and you've got a deal." Ernest shrugged. "So I'm a little impatient."

"A little?" She managed a chuckle. "What say we split the difference and make it twenty-five?"

"Deal." He shook her hand then disappeared down the hall. "Don't be late," echoed along with his retreating footsteps.

"Twenty-five minutes," she said with a chuckle. How that man could make her smile. If only she could be sure that he would accept Ellen, she might feel better about their growing relationship.

Until she knew the answer to that question, she really couldn't get her hopes up that there would be something between them. Her first responsibility was to Ellen. To fall in love with a man who wouldn't love her daughter as his own was unacceptable.

Unfortunately, she'd heard enough comments from Ernest

to make her wonder what his reaction would be.

Tears burned the corners of her eyes, and she dabbed at them with Ernest's handkerchief. Holding the starched white cloth to her nose, she inhaled the masculine scent she'd come to associate with Ernest.

"Miss Lamont?" A sharp rap at the door followed her landlady's voice. "Miss Lamont, you in there?"

Gen opened the door. "Yes, ma'am, I'm here. What's wrong?"

"There's another phone call for you," she said. "Same lady who called last night."

A few minutes later, phone in hand, Gen heard the words no mother ever wants to hear. "Your baby's bad sick," Big Mama said. "You ought to come quick. I don't rightly know what to do with her."

When Gen hung up the phone, she was trembling. Rather than answer her landlady's questions, she turned and ran from the formal parlor where the house's only phone sat. Taking the stairs two at a time, she threw open the door to her room and raced for the suitcase. Ten minutes later, she was heading toward the five-and-dime, a full suitcase in hand.

Leaving the case by the back door, she walked inside, bent on making Lester understand the enormity of the emergency. "So you see, I have a sick relative," she told him when she found him sitting at the soda fountain. "It can't be helped. I have to go to her now."

Lester dug at the gap between his front teeth with a bent toothpick, his gaze never breaking with Gen's. "So I'm to believe that you'd come in here and ask me if you can just up and leave town for a spell then come back and have your same job when you're done tending the ailing?"

"That's right," she said. "I'd be much obliged if you'd hold my job here until I get back."

The store manager let the toothpick fall to the ground and wiped the corner of his mouth with a napkin. "And you don't know when that might be?"

She shook her head.

"No idea?"

"No, sir."

He stared at her. She refused to look away. Finally he climbed down off the stool and tossed the napkin on the counter.

"No," he said as he walked away.

"No?" She followed him to the front of the store. "No?" she repeated. "Just like that, you're going to make me choose between a sick relative and my job?"

Lester turned so quick she almost collided with him. "That's right," he said. "Just like that. So what's it going to be? You want to keep your job or what?"

"No, thank you, Mr. Bonfils," she said, her spine straight and her heart beating furiously. "I don't believe I want to keep this job. At least not under the conditions you state. I have a sick family member, and I'm all she has. I have no choice but to go to her." Gen blinked hard to stall the tears. "And when she gets better and I return, I will be praying that there is still work for me here."

"You always did like to pray, didn't you?" He chuckled. "Guess you don't remember what I told you about work not being a place where a body ought to be praying."

"Oh, I remember," she said. "I just don't happen to agree with you."

She turned her back on Lester Bonfils, and the tears released. If only she'd seen Betty or one of the other girls before she walked outside, but none were to be found. Gen walked alone to the bus station and bought a one-way ticket to Latanier, then went back to her room and cleared out what she could of her meager belongings, fitting them into a pillowcase and the empty corners of her suitcase. The rest she would have to come back for someday. Or maybe she would have Betty send them. Right now that decision would have join the other ones in a place where she could take them out and examine them later.

At this moment she could barely decide to blink or to put one foot in front of the other.

Half an hour later, the bus pulled out of New Iberia, leaving the city and, most likely, one disappointed man named Ernest Breaux behind.

It was for the best, Gen decided as she pressed her back into the bus's lumpy seat. She and Ernest didn't really belong together anyway. Too many secrets stood between them.

❧

Ernest sat on the park bench, studying the splinters in his hands and wondering where he'd gone wrong. When Gen didn't show after half an hour, he went back to her place and knocked until the landlady chased him away. All he could get from her as he stood on the sidewalk was that Gen had received a call. From whom, she didn't know, but the voice belonged to a woman.

He went back and sat on the park bench, just in case he'd missed her. After a while, he went to the five-and-dime and found out from Lester that she'd been fired.

Betty was too busy to talk and probably feared for her job if she did. She sent him out to the park to wait until her shift ended and she could go back to the apartment to check things out for herself. Now he sat waiting and hoping, two sandwiches and a broken heart short of a good evening.

"Sorry I'm late," Betty called.

He looked up to see her heading his way. As she settled on the bench beside him, she placed an overlarge handbag at her feet.

"So, what did you find out? Is Genevieve all right?"

"Well," she said. "I don't think you're going to like this."

"What?"

She looked as if she were about to cry, and Ernest's heart sunk. "She's gone, isn't she?"

Betty nodded. "She took all her things and left me an envelope with next month's rent and an apology. Said she couldn't help leaving on short notice, but she had no choice."

"No choice?" He could barely get the words out.

What happened in the minutes after he left her? Had the damage, whatever it was, already been done before he arrived?

That would certainly account for her tired look, but it didn't account for the phone call. At least the voice the landlady heard belonged to a woman. He told this to Betty and waited for her response.

"No, she never got a phone call before," Betty said. "Least not that I knew of." She gave Ernest a direct look. "I don't mean to be nosy, but did you two get into a spat or something? I mean, this isn't like Genevieve. She needed this job too much to up and leave it, and until you came along, it was all she had."

"No, we were getting along fine." Ernest balled his fingers into fists and slammed them into his knees. "I don't have any more idea than you do."

"All I know is that my friend is gone."

And so is my heart.

Ernest rose and thanked Betty before heading back to the sawmill. His boss had given him free rein to work in the spare room next to the shipping office. If he couldn't sleep, he could work on Mrs. Denison's dining set. It might keep his hands busy, even if it did allow his mind to replay the events of the evening over and over.

Thinking about Genevieve leaving should have driven him crazy. Instead, it gave him hope that if he could just wrap his brain around all the facts, maybe he could make sense of them.

In the hours before morning, with a stack of cut lumber behind him, he finally decided a plan for the future was better than worrying about the past. And his plan for the immediate future was to finish the workweek and go home to Latanier.

If Genevieve went anywhere, it was likely she went home. He didn't know for sure where she was, but he certainly knew where to find people who just might know.

When Friday finally came, Ernest was the first one out the gate. He'd stowed clothes for the weekend in the roadster, along with a pimento cheese sandwich for supper. Without delays, he could be standing on Genevieve's front porch before dark.

He made the drive in less time than usual, owing to the fact that he drove faster and much less carefully than ever. The temptation to drive right up to the house was strong, but Ernest decided it would be much better to have the element of surprise in his favor. Whatever rattled Genevieve into running might cause her to take off before he could speak to her.

The quarter-mile driveway was made of hard-packed dirt, evidence that rain had been scarce in these parts. He arrived on the doorstep a bit more dusty for the trip, but no less determined.

After the first series of knocks, he began to think that getting someone to the door might be harder than he expected. The woman who greeted him last time seemed to be nowhere to be found. He backtracked to find the little cabin, this time with no smoke or anything else to indicate the presence of inhabitants.

"Hello there," he called. "*Bonsoir, Madame.* Anyone home?"

The mangy dog shimmied out from under the house and bared his teeth. "Hey there, boy. You the only one here?"

His greeting was met with a growl and raised hackles on the animal's back. Rather than risk losing a limb to go along with his broken heart, he eased away from the house. The dog barked twice then went to sit in front of the screen door.

Thankfully the dog didn't follow Ernest back to the main house. If it had, Ernest might have gone straight back to the car rather than risk one more knock at the door.

As before, his knocks went unanswered. Then a thought occurred. What if something had happened here? What if Genevieve were inside and in need of help?

Ernest pulled back the screen and reached for the doorknob. He'd have a story prepared when he saw her, a good reason why he planned to walk into the Lamont home uninvited.

To his surprise, the door was locked.

He took two steps back and let the screen slam shut. No one locked their doors in Latanier. What would be the reason?

"You there. You one of the Breaux boys?"

Startled, Ernest whirled around looking for the source of the unfamiliar female voice. No one was in sight.

"Up here."

He turned back around to face the house. Then he saw her. A woman in a set of oversized men's pajamas stood in an upstairs window.

"You the oldest of the bunch?" she called.

"Yes, ma'am," he said. "I'm Ernest. Ernest Breaux."

sixteen

Friday, May 26

"Thank you for seeing us this morning, Dr. Villare." Gen cuddled the blanket-wrapped baby one more time and handed her over to the doctor.

"No thanks necessary," the doctor said. "I wish you'd sent for me. I would have come out to your place rather than cause you to walk to town."

Big Mama shrugged. "It don't make me no never mind." She pointed to Gen. "Even if we had a way to send for you, this girl here wouldn't have been able to sit still and wait. Walking did her good."

That much was true. While her feet hurt, the three-mile walk had given her time to think and pray.

The doctor nodded. "I must apologize, though. I'm here alone today. My nurse is out on sick leave." He winked at Big Mama. "She's my wife, actually, and she just delivered our second son last Sunday."

"Congratulations," Gen said. "Babies are such a blessing from God, aren't they?"

Dr. Villare nodded. "I'll agree with you there. Now, let's see what's ailing this little blessing."

The doctor settled Ellen on the exam table and opened the blanket. Ellen barely registered any notice of the intrusion as the doctor checked her neck and eyes. She complained a bit when he looked into her throat and much more when he took her temperature. With care, the doctor replaced the blanket around her then cradled her in the crook of his arm.

"Her color's a bit pale, but her vitals are good. How long has she had this low-grade fever?"

"The fever's going on four days." Gen looked to Big Mama for agreement. "Starting yesterday, all she wants to do is sleep."

"What's the history of this? When did she start showing signs of illness?"

He looked at Gen, and she turned to Big Mama. If the doctor found it strange that the baby's mother couldn't give a history of the child's illness, he did not let on.

"It started with a runny nose," Big Mama said. "That must have been nigh on a week ago. Just a little inconvenience, I thought. The baby, she didn't seem to take notice of it."

Dr. Villare nodded.

"Well, when she starts to coughing, I said to myself, Big Mama, that little one she's coming down with something."

"What did you do then?" the doctor asked as he handed a sleeping Ellen back to Gen.

"Well, I prayed, naturally, and I put some of that rub Mrs. Lamont likes for clearing her sinuses on the little one's chest. That seemed to help for a bit."

"A bit?" The doctor's eyes narrowed. "How long would you say that was?"

Big Mama seemed to be considering the question. In a moment she nodded. "I'd say that was two days. I thought she was getting better, then little Ellen, she fooled me."

"How so?"

Big Mama shrugged. "Well, she just didn't seem right. She was breathing sort of funny, like little hiccoughs." She demonstrated then waited for the doctor to nod. "And so I picked her up out of the bed and held her up to see what was the matter. Well, sir, she just kept making those little hiccoughs."

"What did you do then?"

"I hightailed it next door to the Widow LeBlanc's house, and I called her mama here to come home. I don't mind telling you, Dr. Villare, I was scared. I thought we were gonna lose our baby girl."

The doctor turned his attention back to Ellen. A few minutes later, after examining her chest and throat once more, he replaced the blanket around Ellen.

"It seems to me that she's got a cold." He reached for a pen and began to scribble notes on a pad of paper. "I think what you heard, ma'am, was her lungs fighting for air."

"Is that serious?"

He looked up from his writing. "It could have been," he said. "But your housekeeper did the right thing. She medicated the baby's chest with ointment and kept her upright so she could breathe better."

Gen cradled her sleeping daughter against her chest. "But all she does is sleep, Doctor. This is not like her." Big Mama echoed the sentiment.

"She's tired. Her body has suffered a trauma, her first infection. All the sleeping is allowing her to heal faster. And the fever, well, that's something we can take care of with medicine." He handed Gen the paper with instructions to have it filled before she headed home. "I would like to have another look at her in a week or so, but only if you think she's taking a turn for the worse."

Gen nodded and passed the paper off to Big Mama. How she would pay for not one doctor visit but two without a job was beyond her. Not that it mattered, for she would go to the ends of the earth to keep her daughter safe and healthy.

"So she's going to be all right?" Tears, her familiar friends, burned her eyes. "My daughter's going to get well?"

The doctor placed his hand on her shoulder and gave her a comforting squeeze. "Your daughter's going to be fine." He smiled. "The first illness is always the hardest—on the parents, that is. I'm sure your husband is worried, so be sure and tell him that if he has any questions, I'd be happy to answer them."

The look that passed between Big Mama and Gen must have caught the doctor's attention. To his credit, he said nothing, but he did turn to his paper and begin scribbling with eyebrows raised.

"Her daddy's dead," Gen blurted out. "That is, I'm a widow. My husband passed on after an unfortunate accident in Texas."

He met her gaze with understanding eyes. "I'm terribly sorry, Mrs. Gallier."

She paused, unsure how to answer. "Thank you," she finally managed to mutter.

"If you don't mind, I'd like to make a few notes on this before you go. I like to keep these sorts of records in case you have to bring her back in." He looked up sharply. "Not that I'm expecting that, mind you."

Gen managed a weak smile. As the doctor worked on his notes, she allowed her gaze to travel around the sparse exam room. The usual jars of bandages and antiseptics greeted her, along with a small photograph tucked into a silver frame on the corner of the doctor's writing desk.

It was a family gathering, a wedding, she realized. To her surprise, there were two brides, one in a gown of white and the other wearing what looked like a bridesmaid's dress.

Dr. Villare noticed her staring and handed her the photograph. "My wedding day," he said by way of explanation.

"Ah," she said as she studied the brides. Both beautiful and both slightly familiar.

"It was quite a day," he said. "Actually it was supposed to be my wife's wedding day. I sort of crashed the party, to my father-in-law's extreme displeasure." He glanced up from his work to judge her surprise, then chuckled. "I suppose I should explain."

"Please do," Gen said.

"Well, you see, my wife's father was set on her staying put here in Latanier, so he arranged a marriage between her and the son of a family friend."

"Do people still do that?"

The doctor smiled. "You've obviously never met her papa. He would have done anything to keep his girl close by. Anyway, he brought this fellow to Latanier to meet my wife, then set a wedding date with the preacher."

"How did he get the man to agree to this?"

"As you can see from the picture, my wife is a beautiful

woman." He set the pen on the desk. "Fortunately for me, so is her sister. To make a long story short, the marriage took place, only the groom chose another bride, my wife's sister."

"How in the world did that happen?" Big Mama asked.

"It almost didn't." The doctor shook his head. "I'd given up on her and taken off with plans to forget her. When I came to my senses, I rode the train home to find a wedding taking place. I guess you can imagine my surprise when I showed up to bust up that wedding and found out the woman wearing the wedding dress and veil was not my wife."

"Land o' Goshen," Big Mama said softly. "Did her mama and papa know about this?"

"It was a surprise to almost everyone except the bride and groom. Those two had gone and applied for their own license. My wife was in on it, of course. She stood at the back of the church and let her sister walk up the aisle dressed as her.

"It would have worked, too, except when I walked up to the altar and begged the bride to reconsider, it wasn't the bride who answered. Her papa about had a fit, but her mama talked some sense into him. He let the wedding go on as planned but with two brides. Of course, he slept with a shotgun by his side and my wife under lock and key until I came back the next day with a proper license and married her all over again and made the union legal. And that time, the wedding vows included a promise from me that I'd never take his daughter from the bayou."

"That's so romantic," Gen said.

The doctor nodded. "I suppose so," he said. "I know it's worked out fine for us. Life's good when the babies are coming and love fills the house, don't you agree?" He paused and an uncomfortable look crossed his face. "Oh, I'm terribly sorry, Mrs. Gallier. That was very insensitive of me."

"No, really," Gen said. "It's fine. And yes, life is good with babies in the house."

This much she knew to be true. The part about love, well, that would have to remain a mystery.

Gen gave the picture another look. Her gaze stopped cold when they fell on the fellow standing to the right of the white-gowned bride.

It couldn't be.

She looked up at the doctor then down at the photograph again. "Dr. Villare, who is this man right here?"

"The tall one? That's my wife's brother, Ernest Breaux."

❧

Ernest drove away from the Lamont place more confused than ever. Although the woman at the window never introduced herself, he assumed she was Genevieve's mother. From what he could tell, she appeared sickly, although her voice sounded plenty strong when she shouted at him to leave the property. Maybe she was the reason Genevieve left in a hurry.

When Ernest begged the woman to tell her daughter he'd been there, she disappeared into the shadows and refused to speak any further. He continued to call her until the mangy dog came to sit at the perimeter of the clearing, giving him the distinct impression he was no longer welcome on the property.

Finally he'd been forced to make the long walk back to his automobile, taking careful glances on occasion to be certain the animal hadn't decided to give chase. He considered heading over to the house to sleep under Mama and Papa's roof, but thought better of it.

A man could get a lot of work done with this much steam to vent. Rather than head to his apartment when the wheels of the roadster hit New Iberia, Ernest guided his car to the sawmill and parked it under the arms of a spreading oak. When the sun rose on Saturday morning, the car was still there, and Ernest had not yet decided to go home.

A chair and two table legs had been created between the late evening hours of Friday and sunrise. If he kept at this pace, he'd have the entire set made before June. That sort of schedule appealed to Ernest. A man who was too busy to think was also too busy to miss anyone.

Right now he missed Genevieve Lamont something awful.

He hadn't found much time to pray over the past months, so busy was he with work and fixing up his automobile, so he remedied that right then. *Funny,* he observed when he'd finished his prayers, *how a few minutes with the Lord makes my outlook a whole lot brighter.*

Ernest slipped into the washroom and threw cold water on his face, then wiped it off with the hem of his shirt. While his stomach complained of emptiness, his eyes longed for sleep. He looked down at the specks of sawdust and smudges of dirt covering his clothing and decided breakfast at any place decent was out of the question.

He checked his watch. A quarter to eleven. Too late for breakfast and too early for lunch anyway.

Shaking off as much of the sawdust as he could, he headed for the roadster and home. He'd get cleaned up, take a little nap, then wake up and grab a bite of late lunch before heading out to the sawmill to work on the dining set some more. Maybe tonight he'd take in a movie down at the Evangeline.

Alone, of course.

Those were his plans. Unfortunately, when he opened his eyes from his little nap he found it was Sunday and he'd missed church.

ə

Gen missed church to catch the early bus back to New Iberia, something that tugged on Gen's conscience something fierce. There was no making up lost time with the Lord, but Gen used the hot, dusty ride to spend time in the Word. The page turned to Psalm 9, and she placed her finger at the beginning of the tenth verse: "And they that know thy name will put their trust in thee: for thou, Lord, hast not forsaken them that seek thee."

Gen closed the Bible and let the warm breeze blow over her face. *Thou, Lord, hast not forsaken them that seek Thee.* Oh, how she wanted to be counted among those seekers. What penalties she and her family had paid for her choice to seek elsewhere.

"It is finished."

Gen nodded. "Yes, Father," she whispered, "it is finished, isn't it?"

In truth, everything seemed to be finished. Her job, her budding relationship with Ernest. Her well-ordered world had come undone, and nothing was certain except the love she felt for her family and her Creator.

"I know that ought to be enough, God, knowing that You have not forsaken me. I wish it was, because then I wouldn't feel so afraid."

She arrived at her rooming house in time to beat Betty home from church. One look at Gen, and Betty enveloped her in a hug, asking no questions.

"Your friend Ernest was here," she said. "He looked. . . desperate." She grasped Gen's hands. "Honey, that man is slap fool in love with you. I wish you could have seen him when Lester told him he fired you. I thought that pompous you-know-what was a goner. It speaks volumes for Ernest Breaux that he didn't deck him right on the spot."

"About Lester." Gen paused. "What do you think he would say if I went and asked for my job back?"

"The truth?"

Gen nodded.

"I think he's going to say no."

seventeen

"No."

Lester's growl rang in her ears. Evidently his pride still smarted from all the times she had turned him down for dates.

"Please, Mr. Bonfils," she said in a voice she could barely control. "You don't understand. I need this job."

He quirked one eyebrow and leered at her. "How *bad* do you *need* this job, Miss Lamont?"

Not that bad.

She sighed and turned to walk away. The only thing worse than begging for her job back was giving Lester Bonfils the satisfaction of seeing her cry.

"Miss Lamont?"

Gen turned and blinked to hide her tears. "Yes, sir?"

He strolled toward her, thumbs in his suspenders. The image of Big Mama's banty rooster came to mind. She fought not to giggle despite the gravity of the circumstances.

"You say you really want this job back?"

"Yes," she said as took a step back and collided with the Alka-Seltzer display. Containers of antacid went spilling to the floor, and Gen scrambled after them.

"Get up," he said with a growl. "I want you to look me in the eye when you answer me."

Gen climbed to her feet and squared her shoulders. With prayer, she managed to make eye contact with her former employer.

"Miss Lamont, you have missed work due to illness twice in the past month yet have shown no sign of having been sick.

Now, without warning, you simply do not show up a third time for work?"

When he paused, she looked away. *Please, God, let him give me my job back.*

Lester placed his hand on her shoulder and squeezed just a bit too tight. "Miss Lamont, you've put me in a bad position with the other employees. If I let you get away with this, soon everyone will want to come and go at will." He slid his hand from her shoulder to clasp the nape of her neck. "A man can't run a business with chaos surrounding him, now can he?"

"No, sir, I don't suppose he can."

An attempt to shrug out of his grasp made Lester grip her tighter. "And yet you're asking me to pretend none of this happened?"

It was all Gen could do to stand rooted in place when everything in her wanted to bolt and run. "You have my word, sir," she said. "It won't happen again."

"Your word?"

His fingers slid from the back of her neck down her spine to rest on the small of her back. Now he stood so close she could smell what he had for breakfast.

For that matter, she could see evidence of egg yolks on his collar.

"Yes, sir," came out sounding like a squeak.

"Did I ever give you the impression that your word was what I wanted?"

"Well, yes, sir. I mean, no, well. . ."

Her voice failed her. From the day he had hired her on at the five-and-dime, Lester Bonfils had been clear about what he wanted from Gen. If she had any questions about what that was, they disappeared when he leaned over and whispered the specifics in her ear.

This time when Gen walked out of the five-and-dime, she was absolutely certain she would never work there again, leastwise not while Lester Bonfils was in charge. She said her good-byes to the few friends she'd made, saving Betty for last.

"You've been a good friend to me, Betty," she said. "Promise me you'll keep in touch."

"I will." Betty linked arms with Gen and steered her toward the front entrance. "Now, let's get you out of here."

Gen shook her head. "You stay put, Betty. I don't want you getting fired for associating with me."

Betty waved away Gen's statement with a sweep of her hand. "That old windbag? He wouldn't dare fire me."

She cast a glance behind Betty to see Lester glaring at them from the back of the store. "What makes you so sure?"

Shrugging, she pointed Gen toward the door. "I know his mother," she said with a grin. "And his wife."

"His *wife*?" She took one last look back at the five-and-dime, then pushed the door open and stepped out into the warm, late-May morning. "I didn't know he was married."

"Evidently he forgets from time to time as well. Looks like I'm going to have to go in there and remind him. Next time he forgets, I'll have his wife reminding him instead. Or maybe I'll let his mother do it." Betty patted Gen's hand. "You don't belong here, honey. I've got a feeling you're going to be just fine. Whatever's got you tied to that little town you came from is calling you home. You need to go to it."

Gen swiped at the tears that had become her perpetual companions. "Not 'it,' " she said. "Her." At Betty's confused look, she elaborated. "My daughter, Ellen. She was six months old last week. She stays there with Mother and a family friend, and I spend whatever time I manage off with her."

"Oh, honey," Betty said softly. "So that's your secret."

All Gen could do was nod.

"Then I did the right thing in bringing this with me to work this morning." She slipped an envelope from her pocket and placed it in Gen's hand. "You put that away for now. Someday you might need it."

"What is it?"

Betty shook her head. "Let me have my secrets, too, won't you?"

"Of course," was all she could manage.

Gen parted with Betty amid many tears and promises that Betty would come to visit soon.

As Gen walked one last time from the five-and-dime to the rooming house, she thought about another promise, one that Big Mama failed to get her to make. Now that Dr. Villare had seen Ellen, it was but a matter of time before the secret of her daughter's birth was out. While Big Mama thought it best to beat the news to Ernest and tell him herself, Gen couldn't make herself agree.

"Genevieve?"

She stumbled to a halt and looked up to see Ernest Breaux sitting on the steps outside the rooming house. She smoothed her hair back and cast an embarrassed glance at the wrinkled mess her dress had become.

"Ernest, what are you doing here?"

He rose and greeted her, at first touching her sleeve, then entwining his fingers with hers. "Where have you been?" he asked, his voice husky. "I looked for you everywhere."

Silence was all she could manage. To speak might mean to say too much, or worse, to say too little.

"I don't care where you've been. I just know I can't ever let you go again." Ernest brought her fingers to his lips and gently kissed them. "Promise me."

Another promise requested. Another promise she could not make.

"Ernest," she whispered. "Please. Don't." When she looked into his eyes, she could swear she felt her heart break. "I can't."

He released his grip, then grasped her wrist and pulled her into his embrace. "Whatever's wrong, I swear I'll fix it. Just tell me what it is."

She shook her head then rested her cheek against his chest. "I can't," she repeated.

"No, sweetheart," he said, his voice a soft rumble. "You can. You just have to trust me first."

Trust. The same issue she had with the Lord.

And they that know thy name will put their trust in thee: for thou, Lord, hast not forsaken them that seek thee.

Trust. Yes, someday in the Lord's own time, she knew she would have to learn to trust again. *Please, Lord, not today. Not Ernest Breaux.*

Ernest seemed content to stand on the steps and hold her, oblivious to the activity surrounding them. How long they stood that way, Gen had no idea. She let the beating of Ernest's heart lull her into a calm she had no business feeling.

Then he took her by the hand and led her away, down the steps and across the street to the park bench where they were to have last met. Settling her on the bench, he knelt in front of her and touched her chin with his thumb.

"Genevieve Lamont," he said gently, "I don't claim to be a smart man, and I'm sure not the smoothest talker there is, but I've got something to tell you, and I'm just going to say it plain. Is that all right with you?"

She nodded.

"All right then." He paused to remove his cap. "Genevieve, I might be speaking out of turn here, but ever since I met you, I have felt like you were something special. I don't know any other way to say it. I love you, Genevieve Lamont, and it took me thinking I might not ever find you again to make me see it."

"Oh, Ernest," she said as tears constricted her throat.

She loved him, too. She'd known it far too long to deny the truth of it. Yet she could never give that love, no matter how strong, to a man who would not love Ellen, too.

Trust.

Gen felt the word settle deep into her spirit, massaging the fear that held her voice captive. If the Lord meant her to love Ernest Breaux, she would have to be honest with him. And she would have to trust that the Lord would guide her words.

"Ernest," she said softly. "I need to tell you something. After I finish, I don't want you to say anything. Can you do that?"

He looked confused. "I'll try," he said. "That's the best I can say."

"Fair enough."

Genevieve looked away, thankful for once that her poor vision caused the world around her to seem a swirl of colors. It made anything besides Ernest's face easier to ignore.

"I need you to pray about what you hear and then see what God's telling you to do." She forced her attention back on Ernest. "I don't want your sympathy, Ernest, just remember that."

When he nodded and grasped her hands in his, she began, "It all started when I fell for a man who promised me the world. I married him and followed him all the way to Texas believing those promises." She paused. "Even when he hit me."

Ernest's jaw clenched, but he said nothing. His grasp of Gen's fingers loosened.

"Eventually he took off and left me a month behind on the rent and without a penny in my purse. I sold everything I had just to get bus money to come home. It was three days after New Year's when I got there. Turns out I'd just missed my father's funeral."

"Oh, sweetheart," he whispered.

"Mother took to her bed and refused to let me care for her. I wasn't welcome, and she let me know in no uncertain terms. When I'd walk in the front door, she'd head for her room, and the only clothes she would wear were Daddy's pajamas. As long as I was in the house, she'd refuse to come out. I guess you could say she didn't take kindly to my running off like I did. In the one conversation we did have, she blamed me for Daddy's death. Said I'd killed him with grief."

The tears flowed freely now, and so did the words. All the secrets, so long pent up, were fighting one another to be told.

"I finally realized I could do her more good paying the bills and seeing that she had her medications. So I headed to town to try and find work. I felt so awful telling everyone I was Miss Genevieve Lamont when the Lord and the state of Texas had declared me to be Mrs. Alton Gallier."

Ernest winced but said nothing. A moment later he released his grip and rested his hands on his knees.

"Moving to New Iberia was a temporary situation," she continued. "Just something to pay the bills until we could find another way to get by. Little did I know it would be *this* temporary."

"Genevieve?"

"Yes?"

"What happened to your. . ." He seemed to have difficulty saying the word. Finally he managed. "To your husband? Does he know what you're doing?"

"My husband? When I ran home, he stayed in Texas. I found out not too long ago that there had been an accident at the oil field. He left me a widow." She paused. "But that's not all."

Gen stared at Ernest, but he refused to meet her gaze. She looked down at his hands, which were balled into fists.

"He also left me a mother." She reached for him, but he pulled away. "I have a baby girl, Ernest. Her name is Ellen, and she was six months old last week."

Gen sat back and waited for a reaction from Ernest. While she prayed for mercy, she knew she deserved whatever was about to happen.

Ernest stared down at his feet, then swung his gaze up to meet hers. The change in his expression stunned her. He looked at her like he no longer knew her.

"You know how I feel about children, Genevieve."

"Yes, but I thought. . ." Her words sputtered to a halt as her throat closed around them. Somehow she climbed to her feet and made her way back to her room to put the last of her things in the box Betty had set aside for the purpose.

As she worked, she kept a steady watch in the window. *Surely Ernest will be here soon. After all, he loves me. He said so.*

When the last item had been stored away and she could delay her departure no longer, Gen made her trek toward the bus station. As she passed the park bench where a short while ago she'd poured her heart out to the man she loved, she saw that man was gone.

eighteen

Thursday, June 1

Five months after she arrived home from her disastrous marriage to Alton Gallier, Gen awoke in her old room. The sun streamed through starched white curtains, illuminating a room with what Big Mama called the Lord's spotlight.

She sat bolt upright. Being careful not to wake her sleeping daughter, she tiptoed down the hall to start the coffeepot. To her surprise, her mother had beat her to it.

Steeling herself for the inevitable, she inched into the kitchen and waited for her mother to turn around and find her there. "Do you still like yours black, Genevieve?" her mother said instead.

Gen nodded slowly.

"All right then." Mother cinched up Daddy's dressing gown and took herself and her coffee up the back stairs. "Be sure to wash your mug when you finish."

"Yes, ma'am." Genevieve tiptoed to the door and watched her mother disappear around the corner.

"Well, how about that?" she whispered as she returned to the stove to pour a cup of coffee. "Maybe today's going to be special."

Despite the initial excitement of actually hearing Mother speak to her, the day progressed for Gen as each one had since her return to Latanier. After Gen fed and dressed Ellen, she took her daughter outside and laid her on a blanket to play while Gen worked to bring Daddy's garden back to life. All the while, Mother watched from the window, and Gen pretended not to know. At some point Big Mama would call them for lunch, and later, after an afternoon spent doing indoor chores, to supper. Bedtime came far too soon, as did the sunrise.

This routine continued for the better part of June. Every day, Ellen seemed to be getting stronger, and soon she would be pulling up and trying to sit on her own. At least that was Big Mama's prediction.

As for Gen, she hoped her precious baby didn't grow up nearly so fast. Some nights, when she wasn't too tired, she lifted Ellen into her arms and danced a sleepy dance in the dark, pretending they were at a fancy dress ball or that they were characters out of a storybook. Most nights, however, Gen was falling into bed exhausted from trying to eke a season of vegetables from the garden was how the day ended.

Still, in those moments between waking and sleep, Gen often pretended that Ernest would ride up, a valiant white knight on a prancing steed, to rescue her from this world of toil and trials.

In the daylight, her thoughts were more realistic. Logic told her what her dreams would not: It had been nearly a month with no word from Ernest Breaux. He was not coming for her.

That realization caused her to tear into the garden with renewed vigor, pulling weeds and tucking wayward strands of pole bean vines into place while the summer sun beat down on Daddy's old straw hat. She'd taken to wearing the hat a few weeks ago, and the comfort of its shady brim could not be matched.

Besides, if Mother insisted on wearing Daddy's pajamas, why couldn't she don his hat?

A movement caught her attention, and she knew it was her mother at her usual spot in the old straight-backed chair in her bedroom. Nothing out of the ordinary in this; in fact, it had become Mother's routine to awaken from her nap and go to the chair to watch.

Occasionally Gen waved, but never had her mother acknowledged her presence. She'd decided Mother was watching Ellen, who now played happily on her quilt beneath the pecan tree, and simply hadn't seen Gen's wave. Believing this made Mother's snub more bearable.

But as Gen peered from beneath the hat's broad brim, she noticed something odd. In place of Daddy's pajamas, Mother wore a housedress of pale blue sprigged in yellow flowers.

Gen rose and dusted off her hands, then turned to face the open upstairs window. "Mother, why don't you come down and join us? Ellen's crawling everywhere, and I thought you might enjoy watching her explore."

Her mother stood very still, then disappeared into the shadows. Gen waited a moment and went back to her work. To her surprise, a few minutes later Mother stood at the edge of the garden, arms crossed. She only stayed a moment, standing warily in the shadows before beating a path back to the house. The next day, however, Mother actually sat in the chair for a few minutes before sitting on the quilt to play with Ellen.

By the last day of June, Mother not only played with Ellen, but when Big Mama carried the baby inside for a nap, Mother took up a spade and joined Gen in the garden. The pair worked in silence on opposite ends of the row until finally they met in the middle. Mother reached for a dandelion at the same time Gen did, and their fingers touched.

Rather than pull away, Mother paused, then entwined her fingers with Gen's. For a moment, neither spoke. Then Gen noticed her mother was crying.

"Oh, Mother," she whispered. "I'm so sorry."

Mother held her arms out, and Gen fell into them. "Hush now," Mother said. "It's me who should be apologizing."

"You?" Gen leaned back and wiped her eyes with the back of her hand. As soon as she did, she realized her hands were covered in dirt. Her face must be a muddy mess, not that she cared right then.

Mother nodded. "Will you forgive me for behaving so terribly?"

"Only if you will forgive me for running off and hurting you and Daddy."

"Oh, honey," Mother said softly as she smoothed Gen's hair, "it's a new day. Let's not live in the past anymore."

"Why didn't God stop me?" Gen wailed. "He knew what would happen, and He let me go and do it anyway."

Mother held Gen at arm's length and gave her a no-nonsense look that took Gen back to her girlhood. "You've got to let go of that, Genevieve. The Lord didn't make a single one of us to be perfect. He knows and so do I that I've made mistakes." She paused to look away. "Big ones." Returning her attention to Gen, she shook her head. "You can't be going about and asking God to explain Himself."

"What?"

"The Lord, He gave us free will. Now I don't like it, and I know you don't either."

Gen shook her head. "No, I don't. It would be so much better if He would just tell me what to do and then make me do it."

"Oh, honey," Mother said. "It would be easier, that's for sure, but better? I don't think so."

"What do you mean?"

"Well, if the Lord leaves us here because we're still learning to do His will—which I believe He does—then how are we to learn obedience if we aren't given the choice to obey?"

"I never thought of it that way, Mother."

"Well, maybe you ought to." Eyes narrowed, she gave Gen a sideways look. "Have I told you lately that I'm proud of you, Genevieve?"

"Proud of me?" She could barely voice the question for the lump in her throat. "What for? I've done nothing but mess up."

Mother gathered her into her arms again. "You're a strong, brave young woman. I know I wouldn't have had the strength to carry on like you have." Her voice cracked and tears began again. "I'm just so very proud. *Je t'aime, ma fille.*"

"Oh, Mother, I love you, too."

By the time Big Mama called them for supper, they both were a muddy mess. Mother swiped at Gen's eyes with the corner of her apron, then used the other corner to attend to her own face.

"You ladies done lost your minds, I declare for sure," Big Mama said, hands on her hips. "Now the both of you need to get yourselves inside and get presentable."

"Yes, ma'am," Gen said as she gave Big Mama a mock salute.

"Immediately," Mother said, seemingly oblivious to the surprise on Big Mama's face.

Gen watched Mother cross the garden and disappear inside before she smiled at Big Mama. "What do you think got into her?"

"It's the power of prayer, Genny-girl. Prayer and a mother's love. Ain't nothing like it." She shook her finger at Gen. "Now go get cleaned up. You look like you been using mud pies for face paint."

That evening, all traces of mud removed, Gen came downstairs to find Big Mama and Ellen waiting. The baby sat on a blanket on the floor, happily chewing on a biscuit while Big Mama stirred something on the stove. The room smelled like heaven, and it didn't take much for Gen to muster a smile.

And then Mother walked into the room.

She wore pink, a trim housedress with white, daisy-covered buttons marching down the front and a smart pink scarf in her upswept hair. Without comment, Mother scooped Ellen up off the floor and settled with her at the table.

They ate their dinner in silence that night, but the next morning at breakfast, Mother began to talk. She chatted about the weather and the way the tomatoes were tasting so fresh, and then she paused to give Big Mama a direct look.

"I want to thank you, Emmaline, for all you've done for my family."

Big Mama ducked her head. "It wasn't nothin' you haven't done for my family, Miss Rose. Why, I don't know what I would have done without you and Mr. Carl when I lost my Henry."

"Yes, well," Mother said slowly as she reached to put her hand atop Big Mama's, "I appreciate it all the same."

ॐ

Monday, July 3

Ernest closed the door to his room and fell into bed, exhausted. All his hard work at the sawmill was paying off, literally. Not only had he been made foreman of the night crew, but his furniture was the hit of New Iberia. It seemed as though the new Mrs. Denison had told just about anyone who would listen what a wonderful carpenter he was.

Phil had left to spend the holiday at his family's home in Crowley, leaving Ernest to peace and quiet—and too much time to think. While at work, he thought of Genevieve and of the secrets she had spilled that day in the park. He longed to be with her. At night before he fell asleep, he thought of the things he hadn't said to her.

If only he could have both the job and the girl.

Even if he could, there was still the problem of the child. He hadn't changed his mind about becoming a father, but he had an unsettled feeling that wouldn't let go.

With the sawmill officially closed until the fifth of July, Ernest decided to go straight to the source—to his papa—to ask him what it was like giving up so much for what seemed to be so little in return.

After a few hours sleep and a hot bath, Ernest loaded up the roadster and headed home, intent on having a man-to-man talk with Papa. Unfortunately, he stepped out of the car and found a party going on.

"There's my boy. Come here and give your mama a kiss, *Monsieur* Sawmill Foreman," Mama called.

Ernest obliged his mother with a kiss, then shook hands with his father. "I'm proud of you, son. My boy, running the night shift, eh?"

"That's right." Ernest tried to work up some enthusiasm for the topic. Papa must have noticed his lack of excitement because he motioned for Ernest to join him on the porch.

"What is it, son? Something bothering you?"

"I reckon it is." Ernest settled onto the bench nearest the door. "I guess I'm pretty obvious."

"I guess so." Papa sat beside him and stretched his legs out. "The job, it's good?"

"Yes, sir," Ernest said. "I like this job real fine."

"And that side job making furniture, how's that going?"

"Real well." He shrugged. "Right now I'm turning away business 'cause I don't have enough time for all of it."

Papa nodded. "So work's good, and furniture making's good. What's the trouble?"

"Trouble? Well. . .where should I start?"

"At the beginning would be good."

"All right, see, the trouble actually started when I met Genevieve Lamont."

"Don't it always begin with a woman?" Papa said with a chuckle.

"Well, this one did for sure. So here's what happened." When Ernest finished, he leaned back and closed his eyes. "So what do I do, Papa?"

"Looks like you got yourself a problem, son."

"That much I know." Ernest turned to face his father. "What I don't know is how to solve that problem."

"If it were me, I believe I'd pick her a big old mess of flowers and ask her to forgive me. Might even consider begging if it came to it." Papa paused. "But you say you wonder how to solve your problem?"

Ernest nodded.

"Maybe you're not the one with the solution." He pointed skyward. "The heavenly Father, maybe He's the One you should be asking for help."

"I tried that, Papa," Ernest said.

"And what did He say?"

"Nothing I wanted to hear," Ernest said.

The truth was, all his prayers had led him to one conclusion.

He was wrong about babies and families and marriage. Still, he figured there must be some wiggle room in the proclamation.

Ernest was still looking for a way out the next day when he packed his things and headed back toward town. He hadn't reached the main road before the white house on the bayou beckoned.

Maybe he'd just drive by and see if Genevieve was home. Or maybe he'd be smart and head for New Iberia while his sanity and his bachelorhood remained intact.

nineteen

Tuesday, July 4

With Mother feeding Ellen and Big Mama cleaning up the kitchen, Gen had nothing to do but sit and read her book while she waited for the heat of the day to pass. The garden was coming along nicely, and they'd even managed to harvest enough produce to send several bushels of vegetables to the Widow LeBlanc. In return, the woman brought over a burlap bag full of last fall's pecans, which the three of them had been taking turns shelling.

Thanks to the generosity of her former roommate, Betty, there was little need for worry. The envelope she had handed Genevieve on their last day in New Iberia had contained enough money to pay for Mother's medicines for the rest of the year.

As another cloud covered the sun, Gen put her book down and reached for the shelling tool. "Looks like it's going to rain this afternoon, Mother," Gen said.

Mother nodded, more intent on feeding Ellen than worrying about the weather. Gen tossed the empty pecan shells into a paper sack and the meat into a bowl beside her. While her fingers shelled pecans, her mind drifted back to the day she had last seen Ernest Breaux.

She often went to that park bench in her mind. Sometimes she told him the truth and pretended he accepted it, and other times she imagined she hadn't. Neither scenario did much for her, as the only real memory she had was of telling the truth and being rejected for it.

Ellen finished her lunch and strained to climb off her grandmother's lap. Lately, she crawled everywhere and loved to pull up on things. Big Mama declared she would walk early, but Mother said she would probably be late.

Personally, Gen didn't care as long as the little girl stayed healthy.

"What in the world?" Big Mama called. "Look over yonder. They's a body coming up the road."

"Well, I'll be," Mother said. "Is that who I think it is?"

"I believe so, Miss Rose. It do look like him."

"Who?" Gen picked up the spectacles in her lap and fit them on. Even though they once belonged to Daddy, they suited her just fine. Indeed there was someone coming up the road. With the glasses on, Gen could see it was a man.

As he approached, she realized that man was Ernest Breaux.

"Emmaline," Mother said, "I believe you and I have some business inside."

Big Mama came to stand beside Gen. "We do?"

Mother cleared her throat. "Yes, dear, we do."

"Oh, that's right." Big Mama tapped Gen on the arm. "Your mama and I, we got some business inside."

Gen nodded, unable to take her attention from the man now crossing the lawn. The man who she could now see carried a bouquet of buttercups in one hand.

"Land sakes, Miss Rose, looks like the boy done picked those flowers by the side of the road."

"Hush now," Mother said. "Ellen, darling, come with Grandma." When she reached for the baby, Ellen began to cry.

"Let's leave her with her mama," Big Mama said. " 'Sides, we both gonna be watching from the kitchen. It won't do to have to keep an eye on the baby, too," she said with a chuckle.

The screen door slammed behind the two women, and for a moment, all was silent. Gen tore her attention from the approaching Ernest and dug into the pecan sack. If he wanted to show up here after all this time, he sure wasn't going to catch her sitting around waiting for him.

❧

Relief flooded Ernest. After all this time, it looked as though

Genevieve was sitting there waiting for him. A movement at her feet caught his attention. A dark-haired girl crawled about, playing with her mother's apron strings.

He turned his attention to Genevieve, and his heart soared. As he neared the grouping of chairs, he watched her stand and scoop the baby into her arms.

"Afternoon," he said, then cringed. What kind of idiot returns after weeks of silence to say that?

Obviously the kind of idiot who would let her leave in the first place.

"These are for you." He thrust the flowers in her direction, then realized she couldn't take them while holding a baby. Placing them on the table beside the pecan bowl, he thrust his fists into his pockets.

Lord, this was Your idea. Now give me something to say.

"Since when do you wear eyeglasses?"

She shrugged.

All right, Lord, now what?

He looked into the eyes of the baby, and the baby looked back intently. "Hello there, little girl," he said sweetly.

To his surprise, she let out a loud wail.

"Hey now, what's this noise about?" He turned his attention to Genevieve. "What's her name?"

"Ellen," she said over the sound of the baby's cries.

"Ellen?" Ernest reached to take the little girl out of Genevieve's arms. "That's a pretty name for a pretty little girl." He whirled her around, then stopped short and did it again. By the third spin, Ernest was dizzy, and the baby was giggling.

"How did you do that?" Genevieve asked. "She's always fussy this time of day. It's her naptime."

Ernest grinned. "Mine, too, only I decided to come here instead." He set the baby on the ground, and she began crawling toward her blanket. "Will she be all right?"

Gen watched the baby settle on the blanket and begin to chew on a teething ring. "She's fine." She leveled Ernest an unwavering gaze. "Ernest, why are you here? And don't say that you happened to be in the neighborhood."

"Well, there went my first response." He shrugged. "I had to come here," he finally said. "I missed you."

The baby began to make cooing sounds. When Ernest glanced her way, she gave him a broad, toothless grin.

"She likes you," Gen said flatly.

"I've been told I'm a natural with babies," he said. "My brothers and sisters and all my nieces and nephews tend to gravitate to me. I don't know why."

"Yet you don't like them."

"What?" He jerked his attention back to Genevieve. "No, I never said that. I love little kids. It's the responsibility I'm not crazy about."

She sighed. "Then, I repeat: Why are you here, Ernest? Because I come with responsibility, lots of it."

"Genevieve, I'm here because I couldn't stand being anywhere else." His sigh matched hers. "Because everywhere I go, I feel like you've just been there. Because I've been miserable without you."

"Yet you and I don't make a good match, do we? What with you being determined to avoid the whole family thing and me having a daughter." She glanced down at Ellen. "I'm sorry, but has anything changed in that department?"

What could he say? It hadn't. Yet. . .

"I'm working on it." That was the best he could do, and it was the truth. Surely she would recognize that much.

Genevieve nodded and reached to pick up Ellen. "That's great, Ernest," she said. "You let me know when you've got it all worked out."

With that, she turned and walked inside, leaving Ernest and the bouquet of buttercups to wilt in the July sun.

2a

Friday, July 21

Ernest wiped his brow and stepped away from his latest masterpiece, a baby crib for the new arrival the Denisons were expecting come spring. One more stroke of the sandpaper and one more wipe of the cheesecloth, and the piece was complete.

He closed the door to the storage room and locked it, slipping the key into his shirt pocket. For the past two Fridays, Ernest had closed up shop and headed to Latanier to see Genevieve. Each time she'd been cool, icy actually, but today he had plans to thaw the iceberg just a bit.

"Excuse me, Mr. Breaux." Mrs. Denison stood in the hallway. "I was wondering if I might be able to see the crib."

Ernest nodded then unlocked the door and ushered her in. She stood in the doorway in silence so long that he was certain she hated it.

"Oh, I love it," she said softly. "It's perfect."

A young man of no more than six or seven raced into the room. "Honey," she said to the boy, "look what Mr. Breaux made for us."

The boy inspected the crib and pronounced it "swell." With the same speed he used on arrival, he raced out the door.

The boss's wife looked up at Ernest with tears in her eyes. "I always wanted a beautiful crib. Thank you for making this possible." She paused. "If there's ever anything I can do for you, please let me know."

He shook his head. "Your appreciation is plenty. Besides, your husband pays me well. I've got no complaints."

She ran her hand over the polished rail then regarded him with a strange look. "Don't you ever wish this was all you did? Making furniture, I mean?"

Ernest shrugged. "That would be something; I'll admit that for sure, but no, I don't dare wish it. That's a dream that's too big to come true."

Mrs. Denison touched his sleeve. "Mr. Breaux, I am living proof that no dream is too big if you give it to God."

"Dotty, are you in there?"

She gave Ernest a genuine smile. "Speaking of dreams coming true. In here, honey. Come and see the baby bed."

A short while later, Ernest helped to load the bed onto a

truck for delivery to the Denison home. The effort made him a bit later than he intended to leave, but it was worth seeing the boss's wife so happy.

Just before the truck left, Mrs. Denison took him aside. "Mr. Breaux, if you were to have the chance to do nothing but carpentry work, would you take it?"

It didn't take him long to ponder the question and answer it. "You bet, unless the Lord told me otherwise, of course."

Her smile puzzled him, and as he drove toward Latanier, he thought of Mrs. Denison's words.

"No dream is too big if you give it to God," he repeated. "All right, God, if that's so, then I've got a doozy for You."

When he reached the Lamont place, he felt as if a load had been removed from his shoulders. After telling the Lord all about his dreams, he'd pulled over and actually listened as God gave him a few unexpected additions to the list.

First and foremost, he had to tell Genevieve; then he planned to go see Papa and let him know he was right about love and fatherhood. He found Genevieve in the garden, wearing a straw hat, a pair of baggy overalls, and a bright red shirt. A smudge of dirt streaked her cheek, and the first thing he did was use his handkerchief to wipe it away.

As he stood there, staring into the eyes of the only woman he had ever loved, Ernest tried to think of something brilliant to say. Instead, all he could do was stare.

"Something wrong?" she asked as she pushed her silly glasses back into place.

"No." He smiled. "Actually, something is very, very right."

"Oh?"

Ernest dropped to one knee. Everything he wanted in life was right here. Now all he had to do was tell Genevieve that. She would ask about Ellen, and he needed to be prepared to answer.

He'd already asked the Lord to handle that situation when it came up. And to show him how to love a baby girl when he'd promised himself he never would.

"Genevieve Lamont, I have something to say."

"You do?" She looked suitably confused. "What's that?"

"I want you to marry me, Genevieve. I love you and—"

"Land o' Goshen, Genny-girl, come quick." Big Mama came racing across the lawn, a limp Ellen in her arms. "Lord, please save this baby!" she cried.

The child's face was turning blue, and her eyes were wide. She looked as if she wanted to cry, but nothing could come out. The last time he had seen a baby like this, his baby sister had swallowed a bug.

Ernest took the child in his arms and, in a swift motion, pressed on her chest as he had with little Mary.

Nothing happened.

Genevieve had become hysterical, and the two older women raced about in circles.

"Quiet, all of you," he demanded as he tried once again to press the spot beneath the baby's rib cage.

Once again, no response. Now the child's face had darkened to a dusky blue, and her eyes had rolled back in her head.

"Come on, Ellen!" he shouted. "Spit it out."

This time when he pressed the spot, out popped a slightly chewed pecan from the baby's mouth.

He quickly righted her and held her against his chest, his heart racing. Before the baby could cry, Ernest's tears began to fall. Genevieve soon joined him, climbing into his embrace to cling to him until he thought she would never let go.

Later, after his brother-in-law Jeff came by to pronounce the baby fit and fine, Ernest sat outside under the stars staring up at the galaxy. He should go home. It had been a long day, and there was no need for Genevieve to play host to him when she had a baby to take care of.

The baby.

Tears threatened again, and he bit them back. "Thank You, Lord, for saving that precious child and for showing this thickheaded man that he's meant to be a father someday."

"Do you mean it, Ernest?" Genevieve asked as she walked

quietly up to him. "Do you really believe you were meant to be a father?"

He nodded. "I'm sorry it took me so long to figure it out."

Genevieve leaned into his embrace and sighed. "I'm just glad you did."

Ernest kissed the top of her head and swiped at the embarrassing tears still falling. "Me, too, sweetheart," he said. "Me, too."

She looked up at him and smiled. "I believe you asked me a question earlier."

He affected an innocent look. "Did I?"

"You did."

"And?" He released her to drop to one knee. "Would you? Be my wife, I mean. And while I'm at it, do you think Ellen would mind becoming my little girl?"

She smiled and nodded. "Oh, yes," she said. "I will. And I can't speak for Ellen, but I'm pretty sure she'd say yes, too, if she could."

"Do you mind if we don't hold off on tying the knot until she learns to talk? I don't think I can wait that long."

Genevieve smiled. "What do you think of a springtime wedding? I'll need some time to get everything arranged, and of course I'll have to be sure Betty can take time off work. I wouldn't think of having a wedding without her. I wish I could find Dorothy. She was such a dear. I wonder if Betty might be able to track her down. Yes, you know, I'll bet she could—"

Ernest kissed her into silence then stared into her eyes for a long moment. "What say we split the difference and set the date for January?"

twenty

"Papa!"

"Horsey again, Ellie?" Ernest scooped a giggling one-year-old Ellen into his arms and trotted around the churchyard while he waited for Genevieve to finish her gabbing with the choir ladies. In truth, he didn't mind the wait. The more time he spent with little Ellen, the more she wrapped him around her tiny finger.

For good measure, he made a circle around the spot where Genevieve's mother stood in serious conversation with Mama. As he neared the pair, he heard them comparing recipes for pecan pie.

"Since we are going to be family, I suppose I can give you the recipe, Rose," Mama said. "You know, it's just like making regular pecan pie. It's the chocolate and honey that makes the difference."

On purpose he cut a path between the ladies. " 'Scuse us," he said. "The young lady's on a horsey ride."

While Mama shook her head, Genevieve's mother called, "I declare you'll spoil that child rotten, Ernest Breaux."

"I fully intend to, Mrs. Lamont. And I plan to have a good time doing it."

To punctuate his statement, he made the best horse noise he knew how to, sending Ellen into stunned silence. A second later, she recovered and shouted, "Again!"

Of course, he obliged.

Twice more around the churchyard, and then he ground to a halt beside Genevieve's mother, hoisting Ellen off his shoulders and up into the air. He caught her then spun her around and held her to his chest. Oh, how he loved this precious child.

And her mother, well, love was such a poor description of what he felt for Genevieve. Yes, it was love he held in his heart, for sure, but there was more. Something deeper.

Something that felt like forever.

How had he ever thought life was worth living without Ellen and her mother? Times had surely changed since the summer—when he'd almost lost both of them.

But the Lord had been good to forgive his stubborn pride and foolish ways. He could now boast of a side job making furniture that paid more than his foreman's job at the sawmill. If only he could be sure the carpenter work would continue to be steady. But then, the decision was already made.

And they that know thy name will put their trust in thee. . . .

Out of the corner of his eye, he saw Genevieve hug the pastor's wife, a sure sign she'd finished her visiting.

"And speaking of time, it is time for this horsey ride to end, cher. Go see *Grandmère*."

Before the child could complain, he handed her to her grandmother, then made a silly face. Ellen's pout turned into a smile and then a squeal of delight when he tickled her under her chin.

She leaned toward Ernest, arms outstretched. "Papa."

"Papa has to go fetch Mama," he said. "Those church ladies must not have hungry men waiting for their Christmas Eve lunches."

"Or an impatient groom with a Christmas secret he intends to tell his bride today," Mama said.

Mrs. Lamont smiled. "Do you know how hard it was not to spill what I knew to Genevieve? Why, at least twice within my earshot, Big Mama nearly let the cat out of the bag."

"Papa," Ellen repeated, her little hands reaching.

Ernest kissed her plump cheek then made another horse noise. "We'll play later, Ellie, after you go see the Christmas tree."

"That's right, Ellen," Mama said. "We're going to see the

Christmas tree at Mama and Papa's house, and you're going to meet all your cousins and maybe even open a present or two, eh?"

Mama distracted Ellen by pointing to a bird, and as Ernest trotted toward Genevieve, he could hear the little girl trying to make chirping noises.

The breeze had a slight bite to it, indicating tonight's Christmas Eve celebration would be held in front of a roaring fire. Some Christmases on the bayou were muggy and warm, so a chilly yuletide was a blessing indeed.

He reached Genevieve in a few steps and swept her into his arms. Oh, yes, there were so many blessings this Christmas.

"Well, now," Genevieve said when he released her. "What was that about?"

"About?" Ernest shrugged. "Nothing." He paused. "All right, I was just thinking about how much I appreciate the Lord blessing me with you, that's all."

A pink tinge decorated her cheeks. "I think that a lot," she said.

"Is that right?" He grasped her hand in his and led her to the roadster. "How about you and I take a Christmas Eve drive while the ladies take care of Ellen?"

Genevieve cast a glance at Ellen then looked back at Ernest. "I would like that very much," she said.

After Ernest helped her into the car, he trotted around to climb inside. The engine started smooth as silk. He sure was going to miss this car.

No, strike that.

He wouldn't miss the roadster at all, not when he'd happily gotten more than enough for her to buy a vehicle more suitable for a growing family. With what was left, he'd made another purchase.

One he now pointed the roadster toward.

Ernest cast a sideways glance at his unsuspecting fiancée and pressed down on the gas pedal. The sooner he got to where he was going, the sooner he would know whether he'd made the biggest mistake of his life.

⋅⋆

"So what's this surprise you've been teasing me with all morning? I declare, I could barely concentrate on the sermon for wondering what you've got up your sleeve."

Ernest slowed the roadster to turn left off the main road. "So, any ideas on what it might be?"

"Nope."

"You sure? That mother of yours likes to talk."

"You mean Mother's in on this?"

"Sure is. Mine, too, and Papa and the boys. I didn't tell Amalie, though. She would have told you for sure."

Gen gave Ernest's arm a playful nudge. He grinned as he captured her hand in his, bringing it to his lips. "No idea at all what your Christmas surprise is?" he asked, his breath warm against the chilled flesh of her fingers.

Eyebrows raised, she yanked her hand away. "Ernest Breaux, you cad. What are you up to?"

He matched her look then slowed to a stop. "Why don't you come out with me and see? If you dare, that is."

"If I dare? Hmmm. Maybe I should stay right here."

Ernest gave her a genuine smile. "I promise this is something you will really want to see." His smile notched down a bit, and he put on a serious look. "I have to tell you I'm a little nervous about this. It's one of those situations where I'm leaning on the Lord and not on my own understanding."

"What are you talking about?"

He pointed over his shoulder. "I can't tell you. I have to show you."

"All right." Genevieve reached for the handle only to find Ernest had opened it before she could manage the feat. Stepping out, she looked around.

"Ernest, where are we?"

"Ah, that's the beauty of this surprise. You don't yet know where we are." He removed his driving cap in a sweeping gesture. "You think you do, but you don't really."

She regarded him with a shake of her head. "Of course, I

know where we are. This is the far north corner of the Widow LeBlanc's place."

"Well, that's what it seems to you." He reached into his pocket and pulled out a handkerchief. "I hope you don't mind but I'm going to have to blindfold you."

Gen took a step back. "Oh, no, you don't. I don't know what you're up to, Ernest, but I am not—"

His pitiful look stopped her protest. "Oh, all right, but remember this is Christmas Eve. If you're bad, there will be nothing but coal in your stocking tomorrow morning."

"That, my darling," he said as he whirled her around to tie the handkerchief over her eyes, "is a risk I am willing to take."

His hands grasped her shoulders as he turned her toward him. Soft lips brushed hers; then he wrapped his arm around her waist. "Hold on tight, sweetheart," he said as he lifted her easily into his arms. "Let's go find out what this Christmas secret is."

A short while later, Ernest came to an abrupt stop. Before he set her feet on the ground, he brushed another kiss across her lips.

Turning her toward him, he lifted the blindfold. She blinked hard and focused on his face.

"Before you turn around, I want to tell you something, Genevieve." He seemed to have trouble speaking. Finally, Ernest cleared his throat. "You know I wasn't always the man I should have been when it came to you and Ellen, but I need you to know that I've done my best to right that wrong."

Gen nodded. "I know that you have."

"Well, like I said, I wasn't the man I should have been, but I believe God's got a plan for us: you, me, and Ellen, that is." He shrugged. "I ought to have prepared some fancy speech, because that's what you deserve, Genevieve. I'm a plain-speaking man, and I don't know a lot of pretty words, so I'll do my best."

"All right," she said slowly.

"Merry Christmas, Genevieve," he said as he placed his hands on her shoulders and slowly turned her around. "I hope you like it. As long as you're agreeable, I'd like to set up housekeeping here with you. After the wedding," he hastily added.

"Oh, Ernest," she whispered as her gaze landed on the little house. "I don't understand. This is ours?" When he nodded, she shook her head. "But this house belongs to the Widow LeBlanc. However did you get her to part with it?"

Ernest shrugged. "You know there are no secrets among bayou people, cher. Mrs. LeBlanc's been looking for an excuse to go live with her daughter in Mississippi."

"I. . ." She walked toward the house, up the steps, and across the wide expanse of porch. "Ours?"

Again, he nodded. "Yours and mine."

"But I thought we'd be living in New Iberia. What happened to your job at the sawmill? You know I won't live here without you." She grasped his arm. "A wife belongs with her husband."

"I agree completely," he said. "That's why, if you'll agree to it, I plan on quitting my job at the sawmill."

Before she could respond, he grasped her hand and led her around to the back of the house. There, situated in a clearing just the other side of the garage, stood a wooden shed.

"Go ahead, Genevieve," Ernest said. "Open the door."

She walked toward the shed alone then doubled back to urge Ernest to accompany her. He seemed inordinately proud of whatever was behind that door, and it just seemed fitting that she should discover the contents of the shed with him at her side.

Giving the door handle a tug, she watched the wood swing open to reveal a tidy workshop. In one corner, a partially completed cradle vied for space beside a pair of matching chairs. A table stood upended with some sort of clamp attached to one leg.

On the opposite wall, shelves held neat rows of paint and tools. A wooden stool painted red waited beside what looked like a drafting table.

The place suited Ernest.

Then she rested her gaze on the object in the center of the room. A rocking chair of beautifully polished wood sat in a place of honor, a roughly tied red bow adorning one arm. Leaning beside it was a hobby horse, its head carved in exquisite detail and a thatch of what looked like real horse hair forming the mane. It, too, sported a red bow.

"Ernest," she said softly as she sank into the rocker, the horse's head in her hand. "This is magnificent."

He knelt beside her. "What's magnificent, sweetheart?"

Gen touched the dark hair of her daughter's toy, then glanced up at Ernest. "This. . .the house. . .you."

Bowing his head, Ernest rested his hand atop Gen's. "Then you're pleased?"

Gen cradled her future husband's chin in her hands then lifted his face to meet hers. A kiss soon followed.

"Just a minute, Mr. Breaux," she said. "I believe there was something you told me long ago that I need to check on."

"What's that?"

"Remember our first date?"

He smiled. "You bought me a Milky Way bar and refused to tell me where you lived."

"And I made you promise not to peek when I walked away."

Ernest kissed her soundly then recaptured her fingers to entwine them with his. "Yes, sweetheart, I remember. What about it?"

"Well," she said. "You told me if I was ever in trouble, I should just whistle and you would save me."

He nodded then began to chuckle when she whistled.

"I think I'm in trouble," she said.

Ernest's puzzled look was absolutely adorable. "Why?" he asked as he tightened his grip on her hand.

"Because this crazy plan of yours is beginning to make sense."

"It is?" His smile was glorious. "You mean you're willing to take me on, even knowing we might have lean times?"

Gen nodded. "We've got each other and the Lord. What else matters?"

epilogue

Friday, November 16, 1934

Ernest set the cheesecloth on the workbench and took two steps back. The cradle was perfect in every way, and Genevieve would love it. Of course, even in her advanced stage of pregnancy, she was agreeable.

One of his favorite things about his wife of ten months was that she made him feel as if he could do no wrong. If only he could convince himself of that.

Times had grown lean, and it was hard not to think of how well he could be taking care of Genevieve and Ellen—and the baby due next month—if he were still working as the foreman down at the sawmill.

And they that know thy name will put their trust in thee: for thou, Lord, hast not forsaken them that seek thee.

"I know, Lord, but I've been holding on to that promise for nigh on a year. I'm all for waiting on You, but those mouths I have to feed aren't going to be able to wait forever." He reached for the cheesecloth and gave the cradle another swipe. "Me, I don't need much, but Lord, if You wouldn't mind, could You send a blessing to my wife and daughter?"

"Ernest Breaux?"

"Oui?"

He stepped out of his workshop to find a familiar visitor standing there. "Well, now, Mrs. Denison. How are you?"

"Very well, thank you," she said. "But the question of the hour is, how are you?"

"Jim-dandy," Ernest said. "You were right, ma'am. There's not a dream too big when you involve God in it."

"You remembered."

"I did indeed. In fact, I wondered what happened to you. How's that baby?"

She smiled. "Perfect in every way, of course."

"Of course."

Mr. Denison stepped into the clearing and strode toward Ernest. "Now you are a sight for sore eyes. I sure do miss you down at the sawmill."

Ernest tried and failed to think of a response. Finally he managed to ask, "How did you find me?"

Mr. Denison pointed to his wife. "Dotty remembered you were from these parts."

"I see."

"I'll get right to the point, Ernest. My wife here's got a project that just may set you over the top."

"Oh?"

"That's right," she said. "A friend of ours in Baton Rouge is opening a restaurant. When he saw your dining room set last week, he had a fit. He wants to talk to you about designing tables for his new place." Her smiled broadened. "And if he likes what you do, which I know he will, then he's going to order new furniture for his other locations." She paused for effect. "All twelve of them. Then there's the hotels he owns. Why, in no time, your work could be nationwide."

"Nationwide." Ernest rocked back on his heels. "Now isn't that something?"

He looked past his guests to see Genevieve walking toward them, Ellen toddling at her side. When Ellen caught sight of him, she picked up speed, wobbling toward him on unsteady legs.

"Papa," she called. "Papa, Papa."

He swept the precious blessing into his arms and kissed her soundly, then turned his attention to her mother. "Genevieve, I'd like you to meet—"

"Dorothy?"

"Genevieve?"

The women began to squeal. "What in the world?" he asked Ellen.

When the noise died down, Genevieve shook her head. "Ernest, this is my friend Dorothy from the five-and-dime."

"No, sweetheart, this is Mrs. Denison, the lady I told you about." He paused. "My boss's wife."

The woman in question giggled. "Oh, this is too much. You're both right."

CLOTHILDE BREAUX'S CHOCOLATE PECAN PIE

5 tablespoons butter
3/4 cup packed brown sugar
1/4 cup honey
1/4 cup pure cane syrup or, if unavailable, molasses
2 teaspoons vanilla extract
2 eggs, lightly beaten
½ cup unsweetened cocoa, sifted
2 teaspoons salt
2 1/4 cups chopped pecans
9-inch pie shell

Heat oven to 350 degrees. Bring butter, brown sugar, honey, and molasses to a boil, stirring constantly. Lower heat and boil for 3 minutes, stirring constantly. Remove from heat and cool 15 to 20 minutes; then add vanilla, eggs, cocoa, and salt. Beat at medium-low speed until thoroughly blended, then fold in pecans and pour into pie shell. Bake at 350 degrees for 45 to 55 minutes. Remove from oven, let cool slightly, and enjoy!

A Letter To Our Readers

Dear Reader:

In order that we might better contribute to your reading enjoyment, we would appreciate your taking a few minutes to respond to the following questions. We welcome your comments and read each form and letter we receive. When completed, please return to the following:

Fiction Editor
Heartsong Presents
PO Box 719
Uhrichsville, Ohio 44683

1. Did you enjoy reading *Bayou Secrets* by Kathleen Y'Barbo?
   ❏ Very much! I would like to see more books by this author!
   ❏ Moderately. I would have enjoyed it more if

   _____

   _____

   _____

2. Are you a member of **Heartsong Presents**? ❏ Yes ❏ No
   If no, where did you purchase this book? _____

   _____

3. How would you rate, on a scale from 1 (poor) to 5 (superior), the cover design? _____

4. On a scale from 1 (poor) to 10 (superior), please rate the following elements.

   _____ Heroine   _____ Plot
   _____ Hero   _____ Inspirational theme
   _____ Setting   _____ Secondary characters

5. These characters were special because? _____

_____

_____

6. How has this book inspired your life? _____

_____

_____

7. What settings would you like to see covered in future
   Heartsong Presents books? _____

_____

_____

8. What are some inspirational themes you would like to see
   treated in future books? _____

_____

_____

9. Would you be interested in reading other **Heartsong
   Presents** titles? ❑ Yes   ❑ No

10. Please check your age range:
     ❑ Under 18   ❑ 18-24
     ❑ 25-34   ❑ 35-45
     ❑ 46-55   ❑ Over 55

Name _____

Occupation _____

Address _____

City, State, Zip_____

Heartsong ❤ng

HEARTSONG PRESENTS TITLES AVAILABLE NOW:

(If ordering from this page, please remember to include it with the order form.)